REMOTE CONTROL

PAULA BERNSTEIN

M&Z PRESS

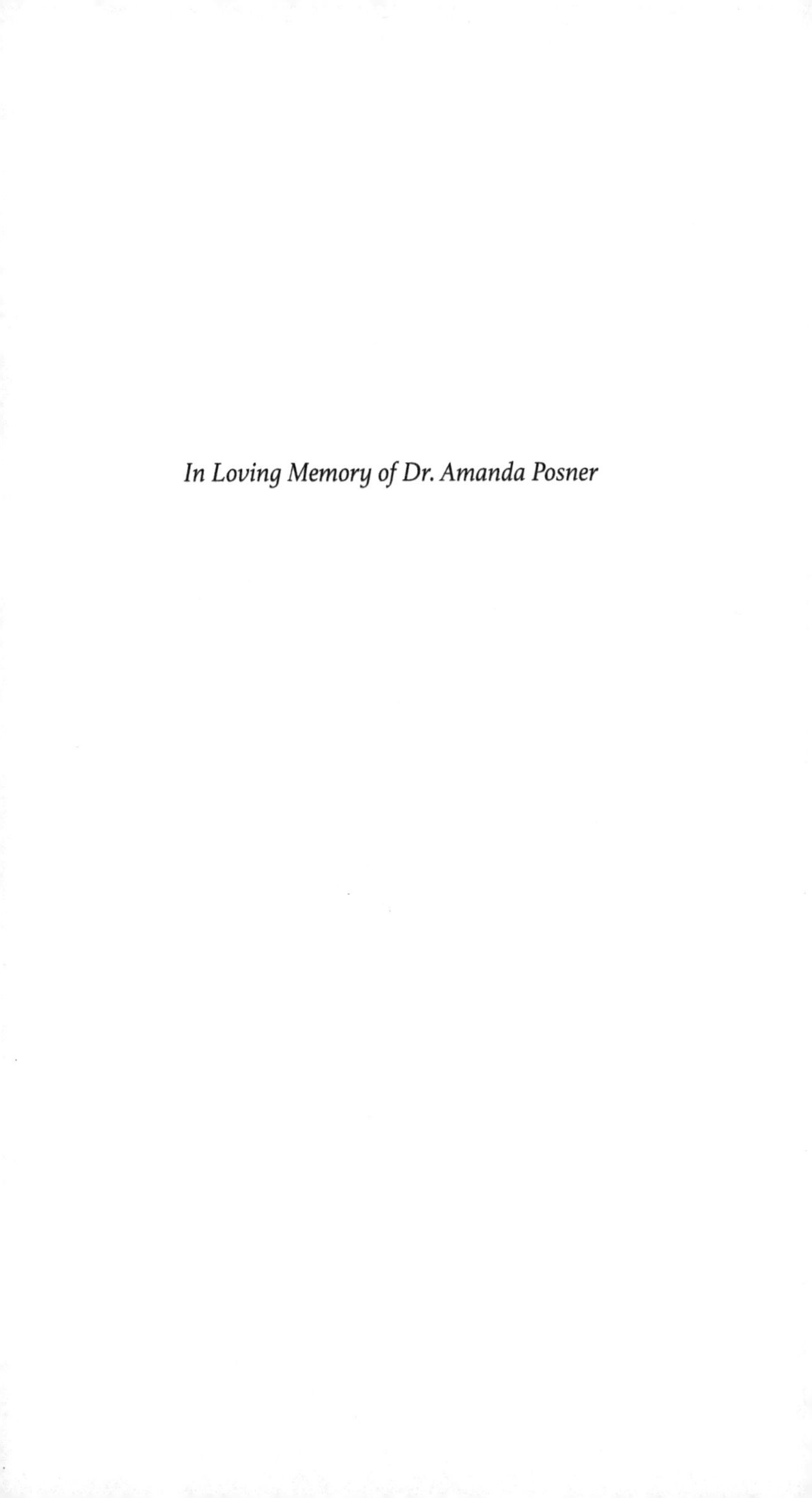

In Loving Memory of Dr. Amanda Posner

1

March 20, 1992, 7:00 a.m.
Arlington, Virginia

COLONEL AVRAM DAVIDSON, MD, PH.D, SAT AT the breakfast table, holding on to a mug of steaming hot, black coffee. His wife Miriam stood behind him, working her thumbs into his rock-hard trapezius muscles. Avram was a commanding figure, over six feet tall, tanned and well-muscled, his curly gray hair closely cropped, his green eyes alert under bushy black brows

"Why are you so tense?" Miriam asked.

"I wouldn't say tense. Terrified is more like it."

"What's going on, or would you have to kill me if you told me?"

Avram laughed. "Today's the day I test my medical device on a live patient. If I fail, the patient could die."

Miriam wrapped her arms around him and kissed the top of his head.

"You aren't going to fail. You've been practicing your technique on pigs for almost a year, and they are all alive and well, and rooting around in their pens. You are an exceptional surgeon, and the patient is lucky to have you. Finish your coffee and go to the O.R."

"Have I ever told you how much I love you?"

"Every day."

———

Avram pulled his car into his dedicated parking space and took a breath before stepping out into the bright, windy morning. He'd taken every possible precaution, but the operating room was a place where the unexpected could always happen. He'd have to be alert every second. The stakes were incalculable, and everyone on his team was counting on him.

He paused outside the main door of DARPA, the Defense Advanced Research Projects Agency, and glanced at his watch. He was early. The wind picked up, and a cloud momentarily covered the sun. With a shiver, he passed through the main entrance and the security check, heading to the operating room. Composing his face into an expression of quiet confidence, he put on his booties and cap, fastened his surgical mask, and walked in.

The elderly man lay on the table. The anesthesia and nursing teams worked on him, starting his I.V. and arterial line, washing his chest with sterile solution, and covering him with drapes. Avram walked over.

"How are you feeling?"

"Nervous."

"We're going to take good care of you, and you and I are going to make history today. Your surgery stands to benefit every veteran with heart disease. I can't thank you enough for trusting us."

"My son's a doctor at Walter Reed. He checked you out and told me you were the best."

Avram nodded at the anesthesiologist, who injected a sedative through the I.V. port. In minutes, the patient was asleep, and a breathing tube was inserted into his bronchus and attached to the anesthesia machine.

"You're good to go," the anesthesiologist said.

The patient, a retired veteran, was the perfect candidate for this very first robotic cardiac bypass surgery. His left main coronary artery was almost completely blocked, but the other major arteries would not require bypass.

Next to the operating table stood the robot, with multi-jointed arms, each fitted with surgical tips. One tip was designed to hold and manipulate the laparoscopic scope and camera. Another grasped tissue, and a third could cut and coagulate it. Avram had named the device ELECTRA, in honor of the very first humanoid robot introduced by Dr. Barnett at the 1939 World's Fair.

The entire project staff was assembled, masked, and gowned: Major McGreavy, the systems software engineer, the anesthesiologist, and the O.R. techs. Another cardiac team was waiting, prepared to do the bypass with a traditional large chest incision, should the robot be unable to complete the procedure in a minimally invasive fashion.

"Ready, sir?" the O.R. tech asked, as she adjusted the lights on the surgical field.

Avram gave the thumbs-up sign. "As ready as I'll ever be."

The tension decreased a fraction as he walked into the adjacent room, removed his mask, and sat at his computer.

At his fingertips were two unique pieces of hardware. They allowed the Colonel's hands to perform cutting and rotating motions. They were also fitted with sensors, enabling him to feel the tissue remotely. Grasping the instrument handles, he adjusted them to position the robot's arms over the patient.

The cardiac surgeons in the operating room had made three tiny incisions on the man's chest and inserted hollow metal tubes through which the robot could place its arms with its instruments.

The laparoscope, a device with a fiber optic light and miniature video camera, was held by the first of the three robotic arms. The others, with their instruments, were inserted through the remaining two tubes.

Avram would operate from his office, constantly watching the video image supplied by the laparoscope's mini camera.

The robotic arm holding the laparoscope moved forward, and gas was inserted to collapse the left lung. The underside of the chest wall came into view. Avram's heart rate sped up, and he could feel beads of sweat forming on his forehead. He took some deep breaths, waited for his pulse to slow down, and made sure his hands were steady. He'd done this procedure on animals more times than he could remember. He knew how to do this. He needed to stay calm.

He traced the path of the left mammary artery on the chest wall, dissected it carefully, freeing a large portion so he could connect it to the coronary artery past the point of blockage. He placed a clamp to control bleeding and cut the artery at its far end.

"I'm ready to bypass," Colonel Davidson said, through the microphone.

The anesthesiologist infused heparin. Avram's next job would be to join the mammary artery to the coronary artery past the point of obstruction. This was the part of the surgery that had always required a large incision dividing the breastbone, and a highly skilled microsurgeon working with magnifying glasses. Performing this procedure in a minimally invasive fashion had been beyond human abilities. ELECTRA changed the odds. At the operating table, the robot paused, and another surgeon made a two-inch incision over the beating heart, exposing the blocked artery.

The first stitch would be critical. The two vessels had to be sewn together with individual sutures, spaced closely enough to prevent leakage. The thread was as fine as a cobweb. Tying surgical knots long-distance was the most challenging part of the procedure. He'd practiced it for months. With precise, delicate motions, he cinched his first knot tight.

One stitch at a time, Avram sutured, tied, and cut his suture, an exercise in hand-eye coordination that left sweat pouring down his forehead.

As the last stitch was placed, he removed his hands from the instruments, took a deep breath, and put them in his lap so that no one could see he was trembling with fatigue and relief. He removed the clamp from the mammary artery, resuming blood flow to the heart, and his repair appeared more perfect than he could ever have accomplished without ELECTRA.

From the operating room came a round of cheering that he could hear through his closed door.

2

———

March 20, 1992, 7:00 p.m.
Arlington, Virginia

AVRAM DID NOT USUALLY JOIN HIS STAFF AT THE get-togethers at The Capitol Bar and Grill in Arlington. He was not a beer drinker, was allergic to peanuts, and hated the cigarette smoke that seemed endemic in bars. However, tonight was a triumphant special occasion. Although he would have much preferred to head home to a glass of Merlot and a thick, juicy steak, he realized the political wisdom of being present at this particular celebration.

A waiter elbowed his way through the bar crowd, carrying a tray with two ice-cold pitchers of beer and mugs for everyone. Another followed him with a bowl of pretzels in one hand and peanuts in the other. The staff crammed into a large booth with cracked red leather seats. Two additional tables had been added to accommodate the group, and the Colonel was seated at the head of one. The waiter put the tray down and started passing out the mugs. McGreavy sat down next to Avram, a bottle in hand.

"In your honor, sir. You've earned it." He popped the cork, and the champagne bubbled to the top and spilled down the side. McGreavy grabbed a mug and poured.

"It's well known you're not a beer fan."

Avram wasn't a fan of this particular brand of cheap champagne either, but he appreciated the gesture. He raised his mug and proposed a toast.

"To a superb team effort and a great team. And let's not forget our patient who was willing to be the first person in the world to be operated on by a robot."

"Hear, hear!"

"Our patient," McGreavy said, "is alive and well. On Monday, another courageous volunteer will be having a double bypass."

"Will our post-op patient go home tomorrow?" someone asked.

"Probably the day after," Avram said. "I don't want anyone to accuse us of doing drive-by cardiac bypass surgery.

Avram sipped his champagne. It was making him dizzy on an empty stomach with all the excitement. In fact, it was making him nauseous. It was probably the smoke. He hadn't been able to stand being in the same room with cigarette smoke since he gave it up ten years ago. He excused himself and went to the bathroom.

The bathroom was hot and only slightly less smoky than the bar. He relieved himself, and the stale, warm scent of urine made his headache worse. His face glared back at him from the mirror over the sink, dark rings under his eyes testifying to the fact that he'd barely slept the night before. He'd better head home while he could still drive. Miriam would fix him up. Hot food, cool sheets, a couple of aspirin, and he'd be fine.

He exited the bathroom, shaking hands on his way out.

"Have a great weekend, everyone. You've earned it."

He stood outside for a few moments, breathing the cold, clear air. They'd probably be there, getting drunk until midnight. Certainly, they'd all have a better time without the boss putting a crimp in their style.

It was almost eight. The working crowd had gone home, the restaurants were full, and the streets were quiet. The bar was on a side street, three blocks from the garage where Avram had parked his car. He took a look around, shoved his hands into his trench coat pockets, and began walking.

His head was pounding. Lights flashed in front of his eyes as if he were having a migraine, but he'd never had one before. He must be coming down with some virus or other. Every muscle in his body ached. Acid regurgitated from his stomach, leaving a sour taste in his throat. He began to cough, trying to control a sudden need to throw up. He never even noticed the two men who stepped out of the alley behind him and hit the back of his skull with the butt of a revolver.

They worked quickly, coming up on either side of him, supporting his sagging body until they'd dragged it out of sight in the alley behind a large dumpster. They opened his coat, checked all his pockets, and emptied them. As they left, one of them attached a silencer to his semiautomatic and fired it into Avram's chest.

3

March 21, 1992, 12:30 a.m.
Arlington, Virginia

THE SECURITY GUARD WAS BORED. THE eleven-to-seven shift at DARPA was always dead. Even the nerdiest of the computer nerds had gone home by the time he came on duty, and the building was dark and quiet. There was nothing to do for eight hours but sit at his security console watching a dozen small pictures of empty hallways.

A faint noise caught his attention, and he watched through the locked glass doors as the familiar white van of the janitorial service pulled up in front of the building. He rolled his chair away from the desk and got slowly to his feet, feeling the stiffness in his knees from all that sitting. The two janitors rolled their carts out of the truck. He opened the front door and waited as they entered.

"Hey, man. How you doin'?" The skinny young black man, his hair in dreadlocks, waved at him.

"Hanging in there, I guess. How's yourself?"

The guard liked Jimmy. He'd been working for the

service for three months now, and he always stopped for a little conversation. The other guy was new tonight. He was big and stocky with pale, pockmarked skin and a wispy mustache.

"Who's your friend?" the guard asked.

"This here's Beau."

The men wheeled the carts around the security station and donned heavy cloth gloves.

"Brought you a little present," Jimmy said.

He bent down and retrieved a cardboard tray. There were three large paper cups of coffee balanced on it.

"The way you like it," Jimmy said. "Hot, black, and caffeinated."

"You sure know how to save a man's life."

The coffee smelled delicious. He sat at his desk and sipped it slowly, savoring the rich, bitter taste.

"Guess we better git workin," Jimmy said, tossing the three empties into the plastic sac lining the garbage can. He rang for the elevator.

"We'll be on the second floor," he said. "Ladies' room."

The guard nodded and sat back at his desk, staring at the screens. It was going to be a long evening. He stretched and yawned, supporting his head on his two palms. His lids felt extraordinarily heavy.

***

The janitors took the elevator to the second floor and collected the trash from the ladies' lounge. They looked at their watches and nodded.

Returning to the elevator, they pressed the button for the fourth floor. The door opened on a small lobby with a locked door. Jimmy removed an electronic access card from his pocket and used it. The men rolled the cart through the door into the high-security medical laboratory.

"Sloppy security," Jimmy said. His homeboy accent was completely gone. "Let's hope the computer security is equally sloppy."

The office containing the workstation had a separate access card. Jimmy had that one as well. He flipped on the light and turned on the computer. Then he removed a blank disc from his coverall pocket and inserted it. The screen gave a login prompt. He typed CYBER.

Password, the screen responded.

Jimmy entered a six-letter sequence. The software came online, and he scanned the menu for a backup function and started the process. It was a large software program and would take a good fifteen minutes to upload. In the meantime, they could be doing something else useful.

Jimmy reached into the depths of the garbage can, removed a metal tool kit, and handed it to Beau. Beau put on a pair of shoe covers and surgical gloves.

The room adjacent to the office looked identical to a hospital operating room with one exception. A device of steel and aluminum stood next to the table, long, multi-jointed arms hanging down, wire connections leading to the computer next door. It made Jimmy think of an obscene spider.

He hoped the boss was right about its value. Jimmy had devoted three months of his life to cleaning out trash cans to get hold of it.

"Don't disconnect any wires until the backup is complete," Jimmy said.

Beau waited until Jimmy retrieved the backup disc and began erasing the file from the computer's hard disc. Then he disconnected all the wires.

The device was remarkably light, its aluminum and titanium arms combining strength and mobility. The two men covered it with a black plastic tarp and placed it gently in the can, covered by the trash bags previously retrieved from the ladies' lounge.

One more detail, and they were done. The backup discs for the software were the final target. The likely locations were the locked file cabinet or the locked desk. Jimmy removed a set of picks from his back pocket. The cabinet's bottom drawer held the backups, neatly labeled with dates. He took them all and relocked the cabinet.

They took the elevator down to the lobby, and Beau drew a semiautomatic as the car slowed. The guard was still seated at the security desk, his head pillowed in his arms. He was snoring gently. He didn't move as the men brought their carts to the front entrance.

"Should I waste him?" Beau asked. "He can describe us." He put the gun to the guard's head.

"Nah. The stuff I put in the coffee will take care of it. He won't wake up tomorrow morning."

The men opened the door, rolled the cart up the ramp into their van, and drove off. The security guard continued to snore, his breaths coming further apart and more labored, until they ceased altogether.

4

―――――

March 21, 4:30 a.m.

Arlington, Virginia

ALANNA DAVIDSON AND HER MOTHER, MIRIAM, sat in the waiting room of the Virginia Hospital Center, waiting for the surgeons.

Miriam got up, walked to the vending machine, and brought back yet another paper cup of black, bitter coffee.

"It's been three hours. I can't stand this much longer." She took a sip.

Alanna reached over and took the cup from her mother's hand. "Caffeine is only going to make you more anxious than you already are."

"I can't believe this is happening. Your father was jubilant when he called me. His surgery went perfectly, and they were going out to celebrate."

Alanna had been celebrating as well when she received her mother's frantic call. The medical residency match results had come out, and she'd gotten her first choice, the prestigious OB-GYN program at Memorial Hospital in Los

Angeles. She'd spent her life on the East Coast, close to Washington, DC, and she'd wanted a West Coast adventure.

What if Avram died in surgery? It was hard enough for both her parents to care for her older brother. How could she possibly expect her mother to cope all alone?

A door opened, and a masked surgeon headed in their direction, removing his hat and surgical mask as he approached. He looked exhausted as he pulled up a chair and faced them.

"Mrs. Davidson, your husband is in post-op recovery."

Tears ran down Miriam's cheeks. "Thank God. I was afraid you were going to tell us he didn't make it."

"The bullet entered his chest and shattered two of his thoracic vertebrae. If it had been a few millimeters to the right, it would have hit his aorta. He was lucky. We operated on his spine and put in some hardware to bridge the gap. Unfortunately, there was a crush injury to his spinal cord. We won't know the full extent of the damage until all the swelling subsides."

Alanna mentally translated the surgeon's effort to break the news gently to her mother. It was likely that her father would be paraplegic and confined to a wheelchair. She didn't think her mother could handle that information right now. She could barely handle it.

"Can we see him?" Miriam asked."

"Of course," the surgeon said. "I'll take you to him. We only allow one family member at a time." He glanced at Alanna. "I'm sorry."

"That's okay. I'll wait here. Thank you for saving his life."

As she watched her mother following the surgeon to post-op, she finally allowed her control to slip, and her pain and anger exploded in tears.

5

———

May 30, 1992 , 4:00 p.m.
Arlington, Virginia

ALANNA KNOCKED ON THE DOOR OF HER father's room at the nursing home, her mother standing behind her. Every time she visited him, she hated the place more. It was so depressing and institutional, even if it was reputed to be the best rehabilitation facility in Arlington. No wonder her father was so depressed. They couldn't wait for his discharge.

"Come in."

Avram was seated in his electric wheelchair, reading glasses perched on his prominent nose, perusing the Washington Post.

"Good morning, darling." Miriam kissed his cheek. "I brought you croissants from your favorite bakery."

"Thank God. I'm not going to miss the food when I get out of this place."

"Dad, have you heard anything yet from the FBI or the Arlington Police Department?"

Avram's face fell. "Not a word. The FBI took over both investigations when they discovered that my access code was used to enter the lab, hours after I was shot. It had to be an inside job. Whoever stole the robot knew exactly what they were after."

"Can you recreate it?" Miriam asked.

"Not without funding, and the government isn't planning to provide it. The powers that be just notified me that I've been placed on mandatory retirement and disability." A tear rolled down his cheek. "Even if they decide to rebuild the robot, they won't put a paraplegic surgeon in charge."

"Oh, sweetheart." Miriam gave him a long hug.

"I'm so sorry, Dad," Alanna said.

Avram grabbed a tissue and wiped his eyes.

"We do have some good news," Miriam said. "The house is all ready for you. We have ramps and railings, and I've removed all the area rugs and rearranged the furniture to make it easy for you to navigate. The shower is now wheelchair friendly and they just installed the stair lift, so you can go up to the bedroom."

Alanna knew how much effort had gone into the renovation, and how painful it had been for her mother to sell the antique rugs she and Avram had acquired on their many travels to the Middle East decades ago. The rooms looked bare and forlorn.

"I can't wait to have you home," Miriam said. "I'm going to interview some daytime caregivers to help you with transferring and with the bathroom."

"Will everything be ready in time for Alanna's graduation?" Avram asked.

"Of course," Miriam said.

"I'll be off all of June," Alanna said, so I'll be available for whatever help you need."

"You should plan a vacation," Miriam said. "This may be your last chance to have fun before you leave for California."

"About that," Alanna said. "I've been doing some research. Not all the hospitals in the DC area have filled their slots for their OB-GYN residencies. I'm thinking of transferring to one that's closer to home so I can be more available."

"Absolutely not!" Avram said, in a tone that conveyed he would not be disobeyed. "I won't have my daughter give up one of the most prestigious residencies in the country for some second-rate hospital because of me. What's happened is bad enough without you making it worse."

A look of disappointment crossed Miriam's face. Alanna knew how hard the past few years had been with her brother Sam's mental illness. Having a disabled husband at home would make things far more difficult. Miriam would have her hands full, but she wouldn't argue with her husband.

"I agree with your father, Alanna. I love you for even considering giving up Memorial, but we'd both feel terrible if you did. Go make us proud."

6

———

January 8, 1996, 7:30 a.m.
Los Angeles, California

CHIEF RESIDENT ALANNA DAVIDSON STRIPPED to her underwear, changed to a freshly pressed pair of surgical scrubs, and stared at herself in the women's locker room mirror. She looked exhausted. Dark circles lined her warm brown eyes with their dark brows, and her olive skin looked sallow in the harsh glare of the bathroom light. Every joint and muscle in her body ached. At least she had showered.

She drew her hairbrush through the tangles of her long black hair and twisted it into a ponytail. It was overdue for a wash. She pulled her makeup kit from her purse and applied blush and raspberry-frosted lipstick. A touch of mascara on her long lashes completed her grooming. At least now she looked human enough to make rounds.

Digging in her purse, she located a double-strength Anaprox and swallowed it with a handful of water. Hopefully, it would take care of the joint pains.

She'd lost twenty pounds during her residency. Most of it was due to the exhausting pace of the work, the lack of sleep, and little time to eat a decent meal, but the grief and guilt over her family had certainly contributed. It haunted her, even more than three years later.

The weight loss flattered her face, bringing her cheekbones into sharp relief, but her body felt bony and awkward. She could feel the sharp angles of her hip bones beneath the scrubs, and her breasts had shrunk a bra size. Most of her good clothes were hanging on her, not that it mattered. She rarely had an opportunity to wear them.

Glancing at her watch, she threw her purse in her locker and headed to the post-surgical ward. She needed to see her post-op patients and was due in Labor and Delivery at 7:30 a.m.

Alanna stood at the scrub sink, watching through the window into the operating room as the anesthesiologist placed an epidural for the upcoming cesarean section. Beside her was the patient's obstetrician, Dr. Vincent Swerdlow, Chief of Staff, mask in place, greying hair covered by a paper hood, his surgical blues tight over his pudgy abdomen.

"I'll be glad when this one's over," Swerdlow said, lathering his hairy arms up to the elbow.

Alanna laughed. "I know what you mean. VIP patients are often the most difficult to take care of, even when their pregnancies are routine."

"A good deal is riding on this delivery," Swerdlow said, "so don't screw up."

"I'll do my best."

She felt her face flush.

Swerdlow was a meticulous and skilled surgeon who kept up with new techniques and enjoyed teaching the residents. However, there were moments, like this one, when she wanted to strangle him. She looked forward to the day she graduated and ceased having to defer to all the surgical prima donnas. He was going to be doing most of the surgery, so if anyone screwed up, it was likely to be him.

Alanna bit back the retort that rose in her throat, finished cleaning her nails with the plastic brush, and began soaping her hands.

"I don't think we have anything to worry about. It's a routine Cesarian for a breech," she commented.

"True," Swerdlow said, but it took Lancaster three wives and five IVF attempts to conceive this kid. Not to mention that he's donating five million to the department for a new infertility research center."

Alanna raised her brows. "I didn't know about the donation; only that he was a hospital board member."

"So now you know," Swerdlow said, "The surgery needs to be flawless."

Could Swerdlow be nervous?

Shaking the water from her hands, she followed him back into the operating room.

Belinda Lancaster was lying on her back, a warm blanket over her legs and another across her chest and shoulders, leaving only her belly bare. A nurse tightened a wide black strap over her thighs, scrubbed her abdomen with a cool brown liquid, and placed blue drapes over her. Nicholas

Broder, the anesthesiologist, informed the circulating nurse that the husband could now come into the room.

As Alanna and Swerdlow gowned and gloved, Colin Lancaster entered. A nurse escorted him to a stool near his wife and behind the drapes.

"It's going to be okay, baby," Lancaster reassured Belinda, caressing her blonde hair through her paper bonnet. "Just a few more minutes and we'll be parents."

She smiled at him, the corners of her mouth trembling just slightly, obviously wishing they would get it over with.

Vincent Swerdlow and Alanna took their places on opposite sides of the table.

"Knife."

He made a careful incision through the skin, just below the hairline, and the two of them proceeded through the tissue layers down to the uterus.

"We're almost there," Swerdlow announced. He gripped the scalpel and cut into the uterus, over the baby's rump, stopping a hair's breadth away from the amniotic membranes. He broke the bag of water. Blood and fluid poured over the incision, pooling on the floor.

"Table down," Swerdlow said. "Lots of pressure, Belinda. He's coming."

He slipped a hand into the uterus and under the baby's rump, easing it out of the incision. Alanna grabbed a towel and wrapped the infant from the waist down, elevating the body so that Swerdlow could free the arms. Once only the head remained to be delivered, Alanna applied pressure from above as Swerdlow's hand cupped the infant's face, one finger in his mouth, bending the head forward to complete the birth.

"He's perfect. A beautiful baby boy." Alanna liked happy

endings. She hoped this one would improve Swerdlow's disposition.

The infant let out a loud, demanding cry. Alanna cut the umbilical cord and held the baby up over the operating table so his parents could see him. She looked at Lancaster, surprised to see tears running down his cheeks. He hadn't struck her as the sort of man who cried. He leaned over and kissed his wife on the cheek.

"Thank you, honey," he whispered.

The two surgeons delivered the placenta and began to close.

7

———

January 8, 1996, 12:45 p.m.
Los Angeles, California

I T WAS AFTER MIDNIGHT, AND THE HOSPITAL was quiet. The fluorescent lighting in the halls shone down on long, empty corridors. The nursing stations were empty except for one ward clerk who sat at her desk, filing lab reports for morning rounds. The phones were silent. The few nurses on duty made their rounds every four hours, checking temperature and blood pressure, and answering the occasional patient who woke in the night needing pain medication. Visitors were gone; patients and babies were sleeping. The only action was in Labor and Delivery at the other end of the hallway.

Belinda Lancaster slept peacefully in her VIP room, among expensive flower arrangements. Her ring finger was adorned with her husband's newest gift, a four-carat pear-shaped diamond, in appreciation of his new son. The baby was in the nursery, attended to by the hospital staff.

A visitor entered Belinda's room, injected the contents of

a small syringe into her I.V. line, and slipped quietly out the door.

Belinda opened her eyes and raised her head. The slight sound had awakened her. She wished the nurses would leave her alone. She was a light sleeper under the best of circumstances, and their constant vigilance made it impossible for her to get any rest. She wanted to roll over, but she couldn't. The I.V. in her arm and her bandaged belly were limiting her mobility. With a sigh, she let her head fall back onto the pillow.

She wasn't feeling well. Her head pounded, and she found it hard to breathe. She tried to take deep, easy breaths, the kind her labor coach had practiced with her, but her lungs didn't want to cooperate. She started to panic.

In the dark, she reached for the call button, which had been at her side when she fell asleep. Her fingers searched the blanket, jerking it involuntarily, causing the call button to fall on the carpeted floor. A wire attached it to the bed. If she could only find the wire, she could retrieve it. Her breaths were coming in ragged gasps now, and the room, what little she could see of it in the dim light, was beginning to spin. She tried to yell for help, but all she could get out was a rasping breath before she fell unconscious.

8

———————

January 9, 1996, 2:10 a.m.
Los Angeles, California

THE HARSH SOUND OF HER BEEPER WOKE Alanna from a deep, dreamless sleep. She groaned and rolled over, feeling, in the dark, for the switch to the bedside lamp in her on-call room. As the chief resident, she usually had at least a few hours of rest on her on-call nights.

The digital clock on the bedside table said ten past two. As she reached for the phone, she became aware of the hospital's public address system making an announcement. It was impossible to make out the words, so she rushed to open the door.

"Code Blue, two Southeast." Two Southeast was postpartum. That must be why they paged her. She slipped her feet into her rubber-soled sandals and sprinted down the corridor. At the far end, she spotted the Code Blue team entering a room and felt a jolt of panic. The room was Belinda Lancaster's.

She elbowed her way past the nurses and residents to

the bedside. Belinda lay flaccid on the bed. Broder, the anesthesiologist, had intubated her and was ventilating. An intern pumped her heart. The cardiologist applied electrodes to her chest.

"Stand back. I'm ready to defibrillate." The intern stopped pumping and got out of the way.

"Now," the cardiologist said.

Belinda's body arched and spasmed. The EKG remained a flat line.

"Again. 200 volts."

"300 volts!"

Still no response. The cardiologist breathed a deep sigh and shook his head. "End code. Time of death, 2:18 a.m.."

Broder stopped ventilating. Alanna turned to the intern. "What in God's name happened here?"

"The nurse went in to take vital signs and found her not breathing. She called a code. I don't know how long it was from the time she stopped breathing to when the nurse found her."

Alanna turned to the nurse. "Any clue?"

The nurse shook her head and handed Alanna the patient's chart.

"She was perfectly fine all evening, Dr. Davidson. She was entertaining a crowd of visitors. Her vital signs at midnight were stable. I went in to check on her I.V. because it was due to be changed and found her like this."

"Could she have had a pulmonary embolus?"

"We won't know unless we do an autopsy and find a clot in her lung," Broder said.

"Has anyone notified Dr. Swerdlow or the patient's husband?" She hoped someone had. It was a job she dreaded.

"We've called the doctor," the nurse replied. "I assume he'll notify the husband."

Alanna left the room, carrying Belinda Lancaster's chart. In her three and a half years of residency, none of the women she'd operated on had ever died. Swerdlow had warned her not to screw up. Her hands were shaking, and she could feel her heart beating a mile a minute. Had she done something wrong during the surgery, or missed something vital when she'd stopped in to see the patient in the early evening?

She sat down and re-read the history, physical, and progress notes. Belinda Lancaster had been a healthy thirty-two-year-old with no prior medical history. The cardiologist was standing in the hallway, reorganizing the emergency cart. Alanna walked up to him and handed him the chart.

"You'll need to write a note."

"Thanks. Rotten luck. We don't do Code Blues down here very often."

"I know," Alanna said. "Most of the time, things go so smoothly that we take it for granted. I still don't understand how this could have happened."

"You know who she is, don't you?" the cardiologist said. "Her husband's on the hospital board. There will be hell to pay for this, even if nothing could have prevented it. I'll bet you he has an entire law firm here by morning."

"I know who she is. I helped Swerdlow perform her surgery this morning. I imagine her poor husband will have other things on his mind besides suing, with a new baby and a dead wife. Swerdlow's going to be incredibly upset."

"Speaking of Swerdlow, I think that's him coming down the hall."

Swerdlow headed toward them as fast as his stubby legs could carry him. The few remaining strands of his gray hair were disheveled. His double chins were vibrating. He was wearing a pair of navy sweats and Nikes.

Swerdlow looked grim. If he had been about to say anything to Alanna, he changed his mind and headed directly into his patient's room. As he reached the door, he paused and beckoned her to join him.

The endotracheal tube made a bizarre silhouette under the sheet covering Belinda Lancaster's body. The floor was covered with debris. Paper covers for surgical gloves and syringes, opened in the frenzy of resuscitation, contrasted with the magnificent, multicolored flowers adorning the room.

The nurse, a wastepaper basket in her hand, was trying to create order out of the chaos. She had detached the I.V. from Belinda's hand, and the pump stood forlornly in the corner.

"What are you doing?" Swerdlow demanded.

"I thought I should clean up before her husband comes. It looks so awful."

She appeared about to start crying. Alanna touched her shoulder gently. "That was thoughtful of you. Dr. Swerdlow wants to examine the body now."

Swerdlow drew the sheet down and stared at Belinda's face. The beautiful socialite they had seen earlier was almost unrecognizable. Her blonde hair was wet and tangled, her skin white and lax. Blue-tinged lips surrounded the breathing tube, and her eyes were wide open as if she were still fighting for breath. Swerdlow tossed the sheet on the floor to examine the rest of the body.

The wound appeared clean and dry, her belly undistended. He parted her legs to find the Foley catheter still in place; no blood in the urine; no excessive bleeding on the maternity pad. Her legs showed no signs of blood clots. With a sigh, he replaced the sheet and turned to Alanna.

"Shock? Pulmonary Embolus? What? How could a perfectly healthy woman be suddenly dead after a completely benign C-section? What the hell did you miss?"

"I don't think I missed anything." *Was that bastard planning to blame her for this disaster?*

"When I came into the room, she was getting CPR," Alanna said. "I have no idea why she had a respiratory arrest. Do you think her husband would agree to an autopsy?"

"Her husband is going to be devastated. How am I going to tell him?" Furious, he strode out of the room.

Alanna didn't answer. Telling the husband was Swerdlow's problem. Protecting herself from the fallout was going to be hers.

9

—————

January 9, 1996, 6:30 a.m.
Los Angeles, California

ALANNA SPLASHED COLD WATER ON HER FACE and debated changing out of her slept-in scrubs. Deciding it wasn't worth the effort, she put on her white coat to hide the wrinkles.

As she turned to go, the door opened and Gabrielle Broder, one of the other senior residents, came in. Gabrielle gave her a wave and a smile. The gorgeous Swedish blonde was Alanna's closest friend and only confidante in the residency program.

"Rough night?" Gabrielle asked. "You look a little tired."

"I'm more than a little tired. We had a Code Blue last night. One of Swerdlow's patients."

"Not Belinda Lancaster?"

"I'm afraid so. You know her?"

"I assisted on one of her in-vitro egg retrievals last year and noticed she was on the surgery schedule yesterday. She was so young and healthy. God, Alanna, how awful. What happened?"

Alanna shook her head. "We don't know yet. I helped Swerdlow with her Cesarean Section. I keep asking myself if I did something wrong."

Gaby touched Alanna's shoulder. "Of course you didn't. How could you even imagine that something you did in a routine Cesarean could have caused an arrest hours later?"

"I know. It still makes me feel awful. I've never had a patient who died. To make it worse, I think Swerdlow will blame me when her husband sues the hospital."

"You've got to figure out why she died before that happens," Gaby said.

"How? I don't have a clue."

"First of all, I'm sure there will be an autopsy. That should tell you something. You should also review the chart, not just the doctor's notes, but the nursing notes, medical administration records, the orders, and anything that could provide a clue. That's what lawyers do. Did you order all the post-surgical prophylactic measures?"

"Of course. Those are standard orders. But you're right. I've got to figure this out before it destroys my career. It's too soon for a visit to the Pathology department. I'll put that on my to-do list for tomorrow and see if they'll share any information."

Gabrielle leaned in and hugged Alanna. "I think we both need a break. How about we find time this weekend when we're not on call? We could go out for Thai food, see a girl movie, lust over the lead actor, and eat chocolate truffles during the film."

"Sounds good," Alanna said. "I certainly don't have any plans. I haven't dated anyone in months. It's never a good idea to date a guy you work with. You can't avoid him if things go south, and who has time to go out and meet anyone else?"

"Join the club. I haven't met anyone worth even having a drink with since I divorced Nick. I wish he hadn't stayed at Memorial. You have no idea how much I hate going into an operating room and seeing his smug face."

Alanna laughed. The lack of suitable men was a frequent topic of conversation.

"I need to get to Labor and Delivery," Gaby said. "Go get yourself some breakfast and let me know when you find out what killed Belinda Lancaster."

10

January 9, 1996, 7:00 a.m.
Los Angeles, California

THE HOSPITAL COFFEE SHOP WAS RELATIVELY empty at seven a.m.. Alanna picked up a discarded copy of the Los Angeles Times, ordered a bagel with cream cheese and a large coffee, and skimmed through the day's assortment of bad news.

The business section caught her eye with an article on the million-dollar salaries currently being commanded by the insurance company executives heading the recent generation of HMOs, and the billions in profits those companies had made and were now investing.

"Trying to ruin your appetite?"

Justin Washington, a fellow senior resident, read over her shoulder. She smiled and motioned for him to join her.

"You're right. I shouldn't aggravate myself so early in the day."

Justin's tall, rangy body slid into the booth opposite her. "Well," he said, "I finally got one job offer for next year."

"Anything appealing?"

The features on Justin's handsome black face grimaced with distaste. "A big MediCal practice. They need another drone."

"Are you going to take it?"

"I hope not. I've interviewed several smaller practices in The South Bay, and I'm hoping one of them comes through."

Alanna took another sip of her coffee. "I get it."

"What about you? Any idea of what you'll be doing next year."

"I don't have anything or anyone keeping me in Los Angeles. I've applied for some laparoscopic surgery fellowships back East. My family is in DC, and I miss them," Alanna said. What she didn't mention was how much they needed her.

"I'm sure you'll get a fellowship. You're a terrific surgeon. By the way, are you interested in a little moonlighting? I just picked up a cushy slot covering the evening shift at one of those Health Web walk-in clinics. They're looking for someone to cover one more night a week. The bucks aren't bad."

"I could use more money, right now. They just raised my rent, and I hate to ask my parents. Who do I call?"

"I'll set it up for you. I'm pretty sure you'll be able to start next week."

11

———————

January 9, 1996, 9:00 a.m.
Los Angeles, California

S HERMAN MAGNUSSEN, CHAIRMAN OF THE Department of
Obstetrics and Gynecology, noticed his private line
ringing as he swept past his secretary and into the sanctuary
of his office. He placed his Gucci briefcase squarely in the
middle of his pristine rosewood desk, seated himself in the
black leather armchair, and waited for the intercom.

"It's Mr. Lancaster's attorney," his secretary said. "Are you
in, Doctor?"

"I'll take it," Magnussen said. He'd spoken with
Lancaster's attorney several times over the past few months,
working out the details of the donation to the department.
The final documents were due to be signed this week.

"Magnussen here."

"Dr. Magnusen, I'm calling on behalf of Mr. Lancaster.
He wishes you to know that he is withdrawing his offer of
five million dollars and is beginning an investigation into
whether criminal negligence on the part of Los Angeles

Memorial and its medical staff is responsible for the death of his wife."

"Death. What are you talking about?"

"Mrs. Lancaster had a cardiac arrest and died last night. Do you mean to tell me that no one bothered to inform you?"

For a moment, Magnussen was speechless.

"I just arrived in my office a moment ago. No one had a chance to inform me of anything. Please give my condolences to Mr. Lancaster. I'm deeply saddened."

"I'll do that, doctor." The voice on the other end was icy. "Our firm will be in touch."

Magnusen replaced his receiver, too stunned for the moment to react. This was a disaster. His eyebrows drew together above his cold blue eyes, and lines of strain clouded his patrician features. How could this have happened without one of his residents notifying him immediately? He'd have someone's hide for this. He slammed his fist on his desk, upsetting a small vase of flowers and tossing pens and papers to the floor.

His secretary opened the door, her eyes wide, her mouth open.

"Get Vincent Swerdlow on the phone."

"Vince. It's Sherman. What's this I hear about Belinda Lancaster? Yesterday you delivered the heir and we've got five million in the bag. This morning, she's dead, he's suing, and we're broke. What the hell did you do during that Caesarean, and why wasn't I notified?"

"I appreciate your support and empathy, Sherman. You weren't notified because she wasn't your patient, and it happened at two in the morning. I was just about to call you."

"I'm referring this case to peer review, and I hope they crucify you."

"You can refer it to the Supreme Court if you like. No one will find any evidence of negligence on my part. Now, if you will excuse me, I have patients to attend to." Swerdlow slammed down the phone.

12

January 9, 1996, 6:30 p.m.
Los Angeles, California

MAGNUSSEN'S DAY CONTINUED TO DETERIORATE. A luncheon meeting of department chairs with hospital administration was called to discuss an offer from Health Web to buy out Los Angeles Memorial Hospital. The discussion rapidly degenerated into a shouting match unprecedented in his experience of executive committee meetings.

He returned to his office with a splitting headache to receive a call from his wife.

"Sherman, don't forget to be home early. We've got to get to the Motion Picture Academy for the charity event."

Shit. He'd forgotten about it. He detested those affairs. He took a Percodan to kill his headache and fell asleep at his desk. It was close to six-thirty, and the administrative offices were empty when he opened his door to head home.

As he stepped out, he saw Lisa Keating, one of the junior

residents, standing just outside his suite, near his secretary's desk.

"I wasn't expecting you," he said.

"Life is full of surprises." As she swung toward him, her white coat flared open. It was amazing how sexy her body was, even in those shapeless scrub suits the residents all wore. She raised her arm and pushed back a lock of her short black hair, the motion drawing his eyes to her breasts.

"There isn't time," Magnussen said. "I was just leaving."

He reached behind him and turned off the bank of lights illuminating the main office.

"There's always time for what you want." She walked toward him. "You look tired. Bad day?"

"Rotten day."

"I can fix that," she whispered, pressing her body against him and urging him back into his office.

Damn the bitch. He couldn't keep his hands off her, and he got hard every time he looked at her. His wife was going to have a fit if he was late.

"You'll feel much better after Dr. Lisa gives you one of her special treatments." Her hand grabbed him through his trousers and started to unzip them. He slipped his hands under her shirt and pinched her nipples hard. She cried out, and he pinched harder.

"How about a managed care cure tonight? Five minutes and out of the hospital."

"God, I can't, baby. I have to go."

Lisa withdrew and straightened his tie.

"I'll take you to lunch tomorrow and make it up to you," he promised.

"It's okay. I'll lock up for you. I have some copying to do."

Magnussen gave her a peck on the cheek, picked up his briefcase, and left.

Lisa waited until she was certain he was gone, then locked the office from the inside. She turned on the copy machine, just in case there were any surprise visitors, slipped into Magnussen's office, and with great efficiency began searching the contents of his desk.

13

January 9, 1996, 9:00 p.m.
Los Angeles, California

THE STRATEGY DINNER MEETING IN THE hospital president's office lasted well into the evening. The table was littered with leftover fettuccine and stale Caesar salad. Lukewarm coffee pots stood at the side of the room.

At the head of the conference table sat Arthur Underwood, the current President and CEO of L.A. Memorial. The late hour was getting to him. He loosened his tie, abandoned the jacket of his navy-blue suit, and rolled up his shirt sleeves. A thin sheen of sweat broke out on his forehead.

To his right sat Vincent Swerdlow, the Chief of Staff. The hospital's Vice President for Finance and the chair of the hospital's board of directors were seated opposite them.

Underwood sat back in his chair, ran a handkerchief over his forehead, and placed his hands squarely on the table. "Well, gentlemen, it is clear this is getting us nowhere, and the hour is late. Let me summarize the gist of our discussion.

"Our VP for finance has presented a grim financial picture that suggests that Memorial may find itself closing unless we can implement many of the changes that form the basis of our objections to Health Web. His analysis is that we have a better chance of survival if we sell and allow the new broom to sweep clean."

Underwood turned to the board president. He started to sweat again and paused to drink some water before speaking.

"Our board president agrees and will recommend to the board that we sell. Dr. Swerdlow strongly opposes any sale of L.A. Memorial to Health Web, and I agree. This hospital has been the mainstay of this community for over fifty years. I would rather see us close than turn into the kind of second-rate, profit-gauging institution that Health Web and its ilk represent."

Underwood's face had begun to turn red. His breath was coming in gasps, and he fell forward over the table, grasping at his chest.

"Arthur, what's wrong?"

Vincent Swerdlow ran to his side and put his fingers on Underwood's carotid pulse.

"The pain," Underwood whispered. "I think it's my heart."

"Call down to the emergency room and have them send a gurney up here, stat. Then call his internist and have him meet us," Swerdlow said. The VP rushed to the inner office and picked up a phone.

"You're going to be okay," Swerdlow soothed. "We'll get you downstairs in a few minutes."

"Vince," Underwood whispered. "Don't let those bastards sell us out while I'm in cardiac intensive care."

14

January 10, 1996, 7:30 a.m.
Los Angeles, California

JEREMY TOBIAS, CLINICAL CHIEF OF GENERAL Surgery, was scrubbing for his first case. Jeremy tried to identify the irritating feeling that had been plaguing the pit of his stomach. Could it be that he was nervous? It wasn't every day he operated on the president of L.A. Memorial Hospital.

Arthur Underwood's cardiologist had called him in at three in the morning after it had become apparent that the president's acute episode was due, not to a heart attack, but to his inflamed gallbladder. Once Underwood realized that he wasn't going to die, he insisted on having his gallbladder removed laparoscopically so he could be back at his desk in a day or two. Jeremy was the medical center's most adroit laparoscopic general surgeon.

Shaking the excess water from his hands, Jeremy entered the operating room to be gowned and gloved. He knew what was at stake in Underwood's rapid recovery and would do his best to bring it about. Jeremy hadn't had a serious complication yet with this procedure, and there was no reason why one should happen now. In another two days, Underwood would be in fighting shape to stop the buyout attempt by Health Web.

15

January 10, 1996, 8:00 a.m.
Los Angeles, California

As she entered the elevator, Alanna saw one of the staff pathologists sipping a large coffee. She smiled at him as she pressed the button for her floor. She remembered noticing him the previous week at the gynecologic pathology conference and thinking he was very good-looking.

"I'm Larry Rosen," he said, smiling back at her. "I joined the pathology department last month."

"Alanna Davidson. I heard you lecture last week. Impressive research you're doing."

"I wish I were doing more of it. At the moment, they have me assigned to autopsies."

Her eyebrows rose with interest. "Are you by any chance doing the one on Belinda Lancaster, the woman who died the night after her Cesarean section?"

"She's first on my schedule this morning."

The elevator door opened, and Alanna held it for a

moment. "I assisted with her surgery. Would you mind if I stopped by later and asked you what you found?"

"Of course not. Any time. I'm usually in my office in the afternoons."

"I'll be there." Alanna released the door, turned, and hurried towards the operating room.

16

January 10, 1996, 8:15 a.m.
Los Angeles, California

ROSEN FINISHED OFF THE LAST OF HIS BLACK coffee, changed to scrubs in the locker room, and entered the hospital morgue.

The corpse of Belinda Lancaster was cold, waxy, and a pale shade of gray. He hated doing autopsies on people his age. It reminded him too much of his mortality. Belinda had been a beautiful woman. He could tell from the bone structure of her face and the thick, tangled mass of blonde hair.

Rosen contemplated the instruments on his Mayo stand and reached for a scalpel. Then he pulled down the sheet that draped her body and began his work. He knew she died from respiratory failure, but the appearance of the lungs still surprised him. They were uniformly filled with fluid and showed signs of hemorrhage. He severed the two main bronchi and the pulmonary vessels and teased them out of the rib cage.

He looked for signs of a large clot, the most likely cause

of sudden death after surgery. He found none. However, the heart looked abnormal with evidence of hemorrhage under the surface membranes. Rosen continued his work, systematically removing and weighing each of the internal organs and dictating his findings into a small cassette he had placed on his instrument stand.

Rosen removed the uterus and examined it for signs of laceration, clotting, or hemorrhage. It appeared normal. He drew a blood sample and sent several tubes for toxicology. Then he began to close.

Afterward, he would begin the most tedious part of the procedure, examining the brain for signs of stroke. Perhaps he could do that after lunch. In the meantime, he would bring the specimens to the pathology laboratory so they could begin processing them into slides. He was completely puzzled and eager to get a microscopic view of Belinda Lancaster's lungs.

17

———

January 10, 1996, 4:00 p.m.
Los Angeles, California

"WHY CAN'T I GO HOME THIS AFTERNOON?" Arthur Underwood demanded. "I thought this was supposed to be an outpatient procedure."

Jeremy grinned. "Because I said so, and today I outrank you. That gallbladder of yours was nasty. I want you to have a few doses of I.V. antibiotics before I send you out of here. Besides, you're an important person to this hospital right now, and you've earned the right to extra special care."

Jeremy's smile was irresistible. Arthur imagined that smile and his classic good looks got Tobias a lot of special favors from the nursing staff. The truth was that Arthur didn't want to go home. He didn't feel energetic enough to get out of bed and go to the bathroom. It wouldn't hurt him at all to stay right here overnight.

Home hadn't been a very welcoming place for quite some time now. Not since his wife died suddenly last year of a stroke. His housekeeper would undoubtedly fuss over him when he returned, but it wasn't the same. He found her chatter irritating, even though she meant well. Better to listen to his doctor for once and give himself a break. He had a big battle ahead of him and had to be in optimal shape.

18

January 10, 1996, 11:30 p.m.
Los Angeles, California

THE I.V. ROOM IN THE SIXTH-FLOOR SATELLITE pharmacy was tucked into a corner across the hall from one of the staff bathrooms. The night pharmacist finished preparing the midnight IV, antibiotic doses, and loaded half of them onto the pharmacy cart. He double-checked to make certain that the narcotic cabinet was locked, and, closing the door behind him, headed in the direction of the medical intensive care unit.

As he turned the corner, the door to the staff bathroom opened, and a figure emerged. Entering the I.V. room, the figure examined each I.V. bag until the right one was found, and made an exchange. The person making the switch, which had taken mere seconds to accomplish, opened the door a crack, slipped into the empty hallway, and disappeared into the stairwell, pausing momentarily to remove a pair of surgical gloves.

19

———

January 11, 1996, 1:00 a.m.
Los Angeles, California

J EREMY TOBIAS GRASPED THE SEVERED, inflamed appendix and popped it into an intra-abdominal plastic bag. He drew the strings taut, pulled the bag to the surface of his half-inch incision, and coaxed it gently out of the abdomen.

"Done," he said, handing the specimen to the scrub tech. "You can close," he told his assistant.

Jeremy stripped his gown and gloves and stepped outside the operating room, removing his hat and mask and running a tired hand through his curly brown mop of hair. God, he was tired. All he wanted was to go home and collapse, but, as long as he was here, he'd better check on his VIP patient. Underwood was probably sound asleep, but Jeremy would feel better once he'd poked his head into the room and checked the chart for vital signs.

The hall was quiet, and the nursing station was deserted as he walked down the hall. The hospital cutbacks had been especially severe on the night shift. They couldn't even afford a ward secretary at night. If a patient rang the nurse call button, there was no one available to answer.

He pushed open Underwood's door a few inches and peered inside. He could see his patient's bulk under the flimsy hospital covers. Something about the sound of his breathing caught Jeremy's attention. It sounded as though he was gasping for air.

He threw open the door and flipped the light switch. Underwood looked toward him. His mouth gaped open, his face red and strained.

Rushing to his side, Jeremy saw that Underwood's face, chest, and arms were covered with huge swollen hives. It looked like the worst anaphylaxis he had ever seen.

"Nurse." He opened the door and screamed at the top of his lungs. "In here, stat."

Two doors opened down the corridor, and slight figures in white uniforms peered out from patient rooms.

"Get me an ampule of epinephrine and a syringe, and the emergency cart. Someone, call the ICU and have them send a gurney down here with a couple of residents. Tell them I need a bed for Arthur Underwood."

A nurse ran into the room with the dose of epinephrine, and Jeremy injected it, followed by a dose of cortisone. Then he intubated his patient.

"What happened?" she asked.

Jeremy looked at the I.V. and disconnected the bag containing the antibiotic. Its label said Vibramycin in bright red. The bag was also labeled with Underwood's name and hospital number.

"He must have reacted to this," he said, "but he has no history of allergy to tetracycline antibiotics. That's why I chose it. He's allergic to Penicillin."

"Could the pharmacy have screwed up?"

"Anything's possible. There's only one way to find out." Jeremy placed the used I.V. bag in a plastic Ziplock and stuffed it in his pocket. "I'll have the lab test it tomorrow."

He was grateful now for that emergency appendectomy. If it hadn't been for that, he'd have been home asleep, and Underwood would be dead.

20

———————

January 11, 1996, 7:15 a.m.
Los Angeles, California

As Alanna pulled her Honda Civic into a space in the physician's parking lot at seven-fifteen a.m., a bright red Lexus coupe pulled in beside her. She recognized Jeremy Tobias as he slipped out of the leather seat and set the car alarm. They fell into step with one another as they walked toward the hospital elevators.

"I heard you removed an important gallbladder yesterday. How's he doing?"

"I wish I could say he's ready for discharge. He had a severe anaphylactic reaction last night to an antibiotic. Fortunately, we found him in time, but it was a close call. He's in SICU. I imagine the word will be all over the hospital by lunchtime."

"What antibiotic?"

"He was getting Vibramycin IV. I've never seen anyone react to it that way."

"That's strange. Are you sure someone didn't put something else in the bottle by mistake?"

"The thought occurred to me," Jeremy said. "I sent what was left off to the lab, just to be sure. Anyway, I've had better days."

They boarded the elevator and rang for their respective floors. Jeremy waved as he got off. He was rather attractive, although he did project that aura of arrogance common in successful surgeons who expect women to fall at their feet. She preferred the Larry Rosen type, men with shy smiles who liked mystery novels. The fact that she was even thinking about this was a good sign.

21

January 15, 1996, 8:30 a.m.
Los Angeles, California

S UZANNE SAUNDERS STOOD NUDE IN FRONT OF her mirror
and scrutinized her body in the harsh glare of the
overhead lights. It had all been downhill from forty. Her
perfect breasts with their generous silicone implants were
beginning to sag, and, thanks to the morons in Congress
with their stupid regulations, one couldn't even get new
implants these days.

Her face wasn't bad from a distance. She'd had her first
facelift at thirty-five and her eyes done shortly thereafter.
The collagen injections helped to fill out the annoying little
wrinkles in her forehead and around her mouth, but they
only lasted a few months. If you looked closely, you could
tell that her neck was beginning to sag again, ever so
slightly.

The worst change was her abdomen, which used to be
flat as a board and which was now lax and covered with
stretch marks. It was the fault of her third husband, who

insisted they have children. Suzanne had been so infatuated with the louse that she agreed, ending up with twin boys and a ruined body at thirty-eight.

It had taken no time to realize that children were little animals and that she was not cut out for motherhood. She'd divorced number three, happily granting him custody of the twins, and divesting her house of every single bit of the child paraphernalia that had cluttered her exquisitely decorated quarters. Now she was going to undo the remainder of the damage.

Sherman Magnussen, her gynecologist, had persuaded her that it was finally time to remove her enlarged, fibroid uterus. His final argument, that a hysterectomy would help her to regain a flat abdomen, made her decision. She insisted that he call in her favorite plastic surgeon for a simultaneous tummy tuck. She'd get everything over with at once and could spend a relaxing week having two of her favorite men dance attendance on her.

Sherman, the poor bastard, had the hots for her for years. He always acted professional, but it was obvious he had a hard-on when he did her pelvic exam. Maybe, once her body was back, she'd give him a little encouragement. After all, she was between husbands now.

Suzanne slipped on some lacy black underwear, a black silk turtleneck, and a pair of jeans, accessorized with an elaborately tooled silver belt and cowboy boots. She had better hurry or she would be late for her pre-op appointment.

22

January 15, 1996, 9:45 a.m.
Los Angeles, California

"AH, DR. KEATING, YOU'RE JUST IN TIME." Magnussen beckoned to her from behind his desk in his private practice suite. Lisa noticed a bleached blonde sitting in the patient chair opposite him.

"Suzanne, I'd like you to meet one of our best residents, Dr. Keating. Lisa, this is Suzanne Saunders. Miss Saunders will be admitted tomorrow for a hysterectomy and abdominoplasty."

"It's an honor to meet you, Miss Saunders. I'm a big fan of yours."

Saunders swiveled in her chair and assessed Lisa before granting her one of those Hollywood smiles that the privileged bestow upon the peons. Lisa was used to it. She'd met celebrities before.

"Dr. Keating will be doing your routine preoperative physical, Suzanne. Do you have any more questions before we examine you and get your blood tests and EKG?"

"I don't think so, Sherman. You run along. We girls can finish up."

Suzanne bestowed a chaste kiss on Magnussen's cheek, and Lisa was amused to see him flush. The rumor among the residents was that Suzanne Saunders was his favorite patient and that he'd wanted to get into her pants for years. He was pathetic.

"If you'll come with me, Miss Saunders, I'll show you where you can change. This won't take long."

While Suzanne was changing, Lisa reviewed the chart. Magnussen always had the residents do his scut work, but Lisa didn't mind. It was a good way to meet his VIP patients, and you never knew when one of them might be useful.

"I just loved you in *Tempestuous*," Lisa said as she listened to Suzanne's lungs. "It has to be my all-time favorite movie. Hollywood makes so few good romantic films."

Suzanne's smile was genuine this time. Flattery always brought out the best side of her. "I couldn't agree more," she purred. "All that violence. I can't imagine why people want to watch brains being blown out."

Lisa palpated Suzanne's abdomen. She could feel the fibroids through the abdominal wall. They were rather impressive.

"I also love *Mack and Mabel*. It's hilarious. The residents watch it when we're on call, between deliveries." Lisa had never watched a full episode of Suzanne's most recent television series, but she'd caught enough segments in the doctor's lounge, so she thought she could fake it if grilled. In truth, she found it asinine.

"I'm glad you enjoyed it," Suzanne said, opening her legs so that Lisa could insert the speculum. "I've always had a gift for comedy. So, tell me, dear, will you be at my surgery tomorrow?"

Lisa withdrew the used speculum and placed it in the sink. "I'd be delighted to be there if you'd like me to assist. Dr. Magnussen always works with one of the residents." She completed the pelvic exam and stripped off her gloves. "I'm all done, Miss Saunders. You can dress now."

"Thank you, my dear." Suzanne sat up and ran a hand through her blonde mane. "I'll be sure to tell Dr. Magnusen what a thorough examination you did."

Lisa left the exam room, closed the door to Sherman's empty consult room, and began dictating the history and physical. When she was done, she picked up the phone and called Sherman's office.

"Sherm, it's Lisa. I have a special request for you from your favorite patient."

23

January 16, 1996, 7:15 a.m.
Los Angeles, California

Alanna deposited her things in the locker room and donned her scrubs, mask, and shoe covers before passing through the door into the operating suite. She was scheduled to assist Sherman Magnussen on a hysterectomy for Suzanne Saunders, a hospital board member and a well-known movie actress. Alanna had never much liked her movies, but you didn't have to act to be a Hollywood sex symbol. All you needed were large enough breasts.

Alanna disliked operating with her department chairman. She always found him cold and demanding, and it was clear that he thought little of the women residents. However, he had insisted on a chief resident for this case, and she was in no position to refuse his request. When she reached the operating room, she noticed Lisa Keating scrubbing at the sink outside.

"Aren't you on obstetrics this month?"

Lisa nodded. "I am, but Suzanne especially wanted me here for her operation, so Sherm asked me to assist him."

"Excuse me? But Dr. Magnussen paged me a week ago to insist I scrub this morning. When did 'Suzanne' make this special request?"

Lisa shrugged and continued scrubbing. "Last night, I believe. You can ask Sherm if you have any questions." She shook the excess water off her hands and walked into the operating room.

Magnussen appeared just then, striding down the corridor, looking confident and authoritative.

"We won't need you this morning, Dr. Davidson. The patient requested Dr. Keating."

"I didn't know they knew one another."

"They met yesterday, in my office, when Miss Saunders came in for her pre-op. She was so impressed with Dr. Keating that she insisted on having her involved. I hope you're not too disappointed."

"Not at all."

Alanna turned on her heel and walked back to the locker room. Bitch. She opened her locker, retrieved her purse, and slammed the door.

"My, my, aren't we peeved this morning?"

Alanna turned and saw Gabrielle changing into surgical clothes.

"What's wrong?"

"Nothing. La Lisa strikes again. I was supposed to assist Magnussen this morning with a hospital board member. I arrived to scrub, and Lisa informed me she'd been requested to take my place by 'Sherm'."

Gaby laughed. "She must give great blow jobs. That's the only reason I can think of for 'Sherm' to be so impressed with her. Try being her chief sometime. She has the largest number of excuses for not doing work I've ever seen, usually having to do with special jobs that Dr. Magnussen has for her. Come on, let's have breakfast. It's quiet in Labor and Delivery, and you could use a break."

They took the stairwell to the ground floor and squeezed into a booth at the back of the hospital coffee shop. Alanna ordered juice and a blueberry muffin.

"Have you heard anything yet from pathology about the autopsy?" Gabrielle asked.

"Not yet. The pathologist is waiting for his slides to come back. I thought I'd stop by later today and see if he has any updates."

"Keep me posted," Gabrielle said.

24

———

January 16, 1996, 8:30 a.m.
Los Angeles, California

THE PATHOLOGY DEPARTMENT SECRETARY TOLD Alanna that Larry Rosen was in his office. She knocked firmly on his door, hoping she wasn't disturbing him.

He answered her knock, looking preoccupied and disheveled. His scrubs were rumpled, and his sandy hair uncombed. He pushed it out of his eyes as he swung the door wider.

"I'm glad you dropped by. This Lancaster case is puzzling me. I've been hoping to talk about it with someone who knows more about obstetrics than I do."

Alanna followed him in, charting her course carefully so as not to disrupt anything.

The office was a tiny cubicle with piles of books, papers, and slide boxes everywhere. Rosen cleared off a chair and motioned for Alanna to sit opposite him at a small table that held a microscope with two sets of binocular viewers. Focusing on a slide, he motioned for her to look.

"These are her lungs. You can see significant swelling, hemorrhage, and inflammation. In addition, if you look in the pulmonary blood vessels, you'll see skin cells throughout the vascular tree. The findings are consistent with an amniotic fluid embolism. What happened during that C-section?"

"Nothing. It was routine surgery. We finished in thirty-five minutes. She had an uneventful recovery and entertained visitors for the rest of the day. Then the nurse walked into her room in the middle of the night and found her in respiratory arrest. The whole picture doesn't make sense. Amniotic fluid embolism is an acute event. She should have had trouble breathing much earlier, not fifteen hours later. I don't get it. Are you sure those are fetal skin cells?"

"I don't have any doubt about the diagnosis. There's no way the patient's skin cells could get into the vascular tree and the lungs. I've just never heard of an amniotic fluid embolism showing up as sudden death after a prolonged period with no symptoms," Larry said.

"I'm at a loss," Alanna said. "I can't think of anything done at the time of surgery that could have caused this."

"Things happen. Sometimes doctors do their best, and patients still die. It doesn't have to be someone's fault."

"I know." She offered him a smile. He was probably right, yet an amniotic fluid embolism was the last thing she'd expected. Something about this whole picture wasn't right.

She pushed back from the table and glanced around the crowded room. One wall was covered in bookshelves, and the medical books and journals were disorganized. The opposite one was decorated with a collage of color travel photographs.

"Did you take these?"

"Guilty as charged. I'm a lousy photographer, but I love to travel."

She examined the photos more closely. "You're quite a good photographer. Where were these taken?"

"Kenya, Nepal, Peru. Mostly during my residency. It's hard to get away for a month when you've got a real job."

"You'll find a way. I love travel too, but I've never tried anything more exotic than Europe." She continued her perusal of the room. The books on the floor, she noticed, weren't medical. Bending down, she retrieved the latest Patricia Cornwell.

"Isn't this a little too much like work, reading a mystery starring a pathologist?"

Larry laughed. "Yeah, but I enjoy them anyway. Have you read that one?"

"I usually wait for them to come out in paperback. I'm short on both money and book space."

"Feel free to borrow anything you like. I've finished all the ones on the floor. I'm usually not so messy, but they've had me working so hard since I got here, I haven't had two minutes to unpack. I promise myself I'll come here some Saturday, but I get seduced by the weather. I trained in Minnesota."

"Well, thanks for the book and the information. If I think of anything that might help, I'll let you know."

She let herself out, smiling as she walked. Rosen was an interesting man. She wanted to read that book, and returning it would give her an excuse to talk to him again.

25

———

January 16, 1996, 9:30 p.m.
Los Angeles, California

S UZANNE SAUNDERS LAY IN HER BED IN THE VIP suite and
inhaled the aroma of the flower arrangements
surrounding her. Her agent, publicist, attorney, and stock-
broker had all sent bouquets to brighten her day. So had the
president of the Diabetes Association and the hospital's
public relations office. It was nice to be appreciated.

Her body was wrapped tightly in a thick elastic wrap
from the bottom of her breasts to the top of her thighs. A
catheter protruded from between her legs, and an I.V. ran
into her left arm.

That nice Dr. Broder from the anesthesia department
came by early in the afternoon to set up her morphine
pump and explained that she could control her dose and
frequency of pain medicine to keep herself comfortable at
all times. He recommended that she use it as soon as she felt
any pain. She'd need less that way, and she couldn't over-

dose herself. The pump limited the amount of drug administered per hour.

Suzanne adjusted her position on the fluffy pillows she'd brought from home and put on her mask and earplugs. Her right hand fingered the remote-control button for the pump. Time for a little sleepy-bye. She wasn't hurting that much, but she'd better give herself a good dose just in case.

She hadn't mentioned to Broder that she took a considerable amount of codeine daily. So useful for menstrual cramps and those migraines she was always getting. Suzanne pressed the button and felt the warm infusion in her veins. It made her feel drowsy and comfortable. She smiled and pressed it twice more for good measure. She wanted to be certain she'd get a good night's sleep.

26

January 17, 1996, 8:30 a.m.
Los Angeles, California

THE DEATH OF WELL-KNOWN ACTRESS Suzanne Saunders after a routine gynecologic surgery made the front page of the Los Angeles Times and all the local tabloids. The hospital's public relations department had no comment except that the incident was being investigated.

An enterprising reporter from People Magazine learned that the hospital's risk management department was talking to the pharmacist who'd prepared the morphine for Miss Saunders' analgesia pump and to the anesthesiologist responsible for it.

An autopsy was in process by the county coroner to determine the exact cause of death. The National Enquirer suggested that Miss Saunders was well known to have a predilection for painkillers and that perhaps, she had supplemented the hospital's dosage with a few things of her own.

Alanna was grateful that Magnussen decided to replace her with Lisa. She had no doubt that if blame were to be assigned somewhere, Magnussen would have assigned it to her.

27

January 18, 1996, 12:00 p.m.
Los Angeles, California

F OR A CITY WITH NEAR-PERFECT WEATHER, LOS Angeles had a paucity of alfresco dining spots. The shaded brick patio at Palma, across the street from Memorial, was a favorite with hospital personnel. At Palma, you could linger for hours over some of the most mediocre food in the city.

Alanna rarely left the hospital at lunchtime, but she couldn't stand to be there one more minute. She had to have a break, and Gabrielle had convinced her to meet for lunch. She was already at a corner table, sipping an iced tea.

"Thanks for suggesting this. The tension around the department is so thick today you could dissect it."

Gabrielle smiled. "I wonder why I bother to read this menu. I always order the spaghetti. At least it's edible."

Alanna ordered a Caesar Salad. "Everyone is incredibly upset about the death of Suzanne Saunders. It looks like an overdose, but those PCA pumps are supposed to be programmed so that can't happen. There's going to be a huge investigation."

"Too many things have been going wrong lately in this hospital," Gabrielle said. "One of our OB nurses is dating a lab tech. She told me that Arthur Underwood accidentally got a dose of Penicillin, to which he is allergic, instead of the antibiotic that was ordered. Someone made a bad mistake."

Alanna took a swallow of Coke. "Maybe it wasn't a mistake? Maybe it was deliberate."

"I'd find that hard to believe. Why would the pharmacist want to kill Arthur Underwood?"

"I'm not implying it was the pharmacist. Don't you find it strange that in the space of less than two weeks, Arthur Underwood is given an antibiotic that he's violently allergic to, the wife of a board member dies of an amniotic fluid embolism fifteen hours after her delivery, and Suzanne Saunders, another board member, dies yesterday of a supposed overdose. If I were a board member at L.A. Memorial, I'd be nervous right now."

Gaby stared at her. "Seriously? It was an amniotic fluid embolism?"

"That's what the slides show. I couldn't believe it either. I have no insight into hospital politics. Can you think of any reason someone might want to harm three board members?" Alanna said.

"Not a clue," Gabrielle said, "but if I were you, I'd keep my suspicions to myself. If something dangerous is going on, you don't want to get in the middle of it."

Gabrielle was probably right about being cautious. It wouldn't do to start any rumors without facts. But she wasn't going to forget about it. She didn't see why she couldn't check into a few things on her own. The more she thought about it, she knew just the place to start.

28

———

January 18, 1996, 2:30 p.m.
Los Angeles, California

LARRY ROSEN WAS IN HIS OFFICE READING A pathology journal when Alanna knocked.

"I'm here to pick your brain if you aren't busy."

"Pick away." Larry put down his journal and waved her to a seat.

"It's about the Belinda Lancaster case."

"You too? Nick Broder was in a few days ago. It's a real puzzle. I did a Medline, trying to find a case report of someone whose onset of symptoms from amniotic fluid embolism occurred as late as hers, and there's nothing like it in the literature."

"I have a thought about that, but you have to promise not to laugh at me and not to repeat it to anyone."

"My lips are sealed. What's your idea?"

"What if her symptoms occurred late because someone deliberately injected amniotic fluid into her IV?"

"You're talking about murder. How would they get the amniotic fluid?"

"There's plenty of it around. We do genetic amniocentesis all the time in the obstetrical clinic. It would be difficult to get a clean sample of Belinda Lancaster's amniotic fluid during surgery because most of it winds up on the floor or all over the drapes, but it would be easy for someone to get hold of another patient's fluid. Is there any way you could match the cell genetics of the cells in Belinda's lung to her son's cord blood sample?"

"I think so. I could isolate enough cells to do a polymerase chain reaction."

"Would you be willing to do the testing?"

Rosen hesitated, and then he nodded. "If it's any consolation, I'm not laughing at you. This isn't the only strange thing going on around here. If you promise me equal secrecy, I'll share another disturbing pathology result."

"I'm all ears."

"They haven't finished Suzanne Saunders' autopsy yet, but we did the toxicology. Her blood level of morphine was the equivalent of an I.V. injection of three hundred milligrams. No wonder the woman stopped breathing."

"I didn't think that kind of overdose could happen with a PCA pump."

"As far as I know, it didn't," Larry said. "Both the pump setting and medication concentration were checked. Either she administered the extra herself, or someone did it for her."

Alanna shuddered. "This is getting frightening. If I should get sick anytime soon, remind me to recuperate at home, will you?"

"Not to worry. Incidentally, did you have a chance to read that book?"

"I'm halfway done. I notice you've straightened up. I can cross the room without tripping on anything."

Larry smiled. "Well, I thought if you were going to make a habit of using my lending library, I wanted you to be able to find things. Look, a whole shelf of mysteries, right next to the New England Journal."

"I can't wait to borrow the next one. I'd better get back to work. Will you let me know when you've done that PCR?"

"I promise."

He held open the door for her, touching her shoulder lightly as she passed through. At least he'd taken her seriously, rather than patronizing her. From now on, she was going to keep her suspicions to herself. If she was right, someone at this hospital was a dangerous killer.

29

——————

January 19, 1996, 10:30 p.m.
Los Angeles, California

ALANNA HAD JUST FINISHED IN THE OPERATING room when her beeper sounded, and she headed for the nearest phone.

"It's Larry. I've found something interesting. Do you have time to stop up?"

"I'll be there in five."

Larry was seated at his desk when Alanna walked in.

"Your hunch was correct. I didn't even need to do a PCR. I did some electron micrographs of the cells to look at the chromosomes before trying to isolate a sample. They all had XX chromosomes. If the event had happened naturally, the cells would have had XY chromosomes because Belinda had a son. The only way female fetal cells could have reached her lungs is if someone injected her with them."

Alanna sat down opposite him. A sudden tense knot had formed in her stomach. "I was hoping you'd prove me wrong, and I could forget about this. Can you isolate enough cells for a PCR? I'll try to find out how many amniocenteses were done in the day or two before this happened and figure out who had access. It would help to know exactly which sample was used."

"Don't you think we should notify the police?" Larry said.

"Yes, I do, but we should first find out everything we can. I wouldn't want the police to think we're both nut cases. Besides, once they start asking questions around the hospital, the person who did this may destroy any evidence left. If we look around quietly, we could discover a few things the police might miss."

"Okay, boss. We'll do it your way."

Alanna opened the door to the antenatal clinic and smiled at Muriel, the ward clerk. Muriel was the motherly sort and considered the residents her special responsibility.

"Is there something I can help you with?" she asked.

"I just need a peek at your appointment book. I'm trying to trace down some lab work."

"Here you go." Muriel handed it over. "Why don't you sit at my desk and look at it while I go to the ladies?"

Alanna took the book and turned to the previous week's appointments. Belinda's death had occurred on a Tuesday. Alanna checked for samples collected on Monday and Tuesday, and from the previous week.

Only three patients had been scheduled for amniocentesis during that time. Alanna copied their names. Then she accessed the computer terminal on Muriel's desk and obtained their hospital numbers. None of the three was currently in the hospital, which meant their charts should be available in Medical Records.

Heading to medical records, she asked the clerk to pull the charts. Two of the tests were genetic amniocenteses run on women who were 15 weeks pregnant. One of the two was going to have a girl. The third amniocentesis had been performed for lung maturity on a diabetic. She had delivered a female infant two days later.

Of the two relevant procedures, one was performed by Lisa Keating, and the other by Gabrielle Broder. In addition to the two physicians, the clinic nurses, the secretary, and the lab technicians all had access to the specimens. There had also been a messenger who brought the samples from the clinic to the lab, but Alanna doubted he was a serious possibility. This murder required some medical sophistication and knowledge, not to mention motive. None of it made much sense.

Her next stop was the amniocentesis lab, a tiny room run by only one senior lab technician. Alanna had known him since her internship and always found him knowledgeable and helpful.

"You wouldn't happen to have some leftover amniotic fluid I could borrow, would you?"

"Last week's specimens are still in the fridge," he said. "Don't take anything past Friday. What are you up to?"

"Just a little chemistry experiment. I'll tell you about it if it works." She opened the refrigerator door and checked the names and dates on the rack of tubes. The two she was seeking were still there, and she slipped them into a plastic bag and into her pocket.

"Do you need these back, or can I use the remainder of the fluid?" Alanna asked.

"I was about to dump everything more than a week old. Help yourself."

She slipped the two tubes into her lab coat pocket. She'd drop them off at Larry's lab and grab her mail from the main office before she took off for the day.

30

———

January 19, 1996, 4:45 p.m.
Los Angeles, California

T HE CERTIFIED LETTER, IN HER MAIL FROM THE OB-GYN office, stopped Alanna cold. She knew what it was without opening it. There was no other possibility when you received certified mail from a lawyer's office.

The letter informed her that Colin Lancaster was suing Vincent Swerdlow, Los Angeles Memorial Hospital, and others, including Alanna, for gross negligence resulting in the death of his wife.

How could this have happened to her? It wasn't her fault. She'd have to tell Dr. Magnussen and the hospital legal office, which handled the residents' malpractice insurance. Everyone would find out, and her reputation would be ruined. Being sued for malpractice was one of the worst things that could happen to a resident.

Everyone would think she was an incompetent doctor. No one would want to practice with her or be her patient. Her career would be over before it got started.

She slipped the letter into her purse and felt her control begin to slip. Tears made their way down her cheeks, and she choked back a sob, wiping her eyes on the sleeve of her white coat.

Glancing at her watch, she made a beeline for the locker room. She had to stop crying and fix her face before her eyes got bloodshot. She was due to start her new moonlighting job tonight, and she had to look professional.

31

January 22, 1996, 7:00 p.m.
Los Angeles, California

U RGENT CARE CENTERS HAD BEEN SPRINGING up all over Los Angeles, the medical residents referring to them contemptuously as "Doc in a Box." Although not widely admired, the centers offered excellent opportunities for supplementing a meager resident income, and many of Alanna's colleagues took advantage of the easy cash they could earn moonlighting.

The clinic in Santa Monica was on Wilshire, perfectly located to attract patients away from the emergency rooms of the city's two main hospitals. Alanna parked her car on the street and entered the front door.

"Can I help you?" A fresh-faced receptionist sat in the window of a large, packed waiting room. There had to be over fifty patients there. Alanna couldn't imagine how she could see them all.

"I'm Dr. Davidson. I'm taking the evening shift here tonight from seven to ten."

"Most doctors park in the lot behind the building and come in the back way. I didn't realize who you were, Doctor. Let me tell Miss Hauptmann you're here."

She picked up the phone, and a moment later, a stout, grey-haired woman in a white nurses' uniform came out of the back office. She held out her hand.

"I'm Miss Hauptmann, the clinic administrator. Follow me, please."

She turned and led Alanna through the door into a long corridor with a nurse's station at one end. Young people in short white coats were escorting patients into examination rooms. There was a physician's consult room at the far end, and Miss Hauptmann opened the door and motioned Alanna to precede her.

"Your office and your white coat are here. You will find pens, paper, prescription pads, and whatever else you need in the desk. The examination rooms are completely equipped. Someone will let you know when there is a patient for you."

"Is it always this busy?" Alanna asked. "I can't imagine how I'll be able to see all those people in three hours."

"They are not all for you. We use nurse practitioners and physician assistants for most patients. You will only see the sickest patients who might need hospital admission."

"Where and how do I admit them?"

"We have several Health Web-affiliated physicians available at the local hospitals. You will find a list of hospitals and doctors you can call in the desk drawer, should you need it. You won't find this job too taxing, I'm sure." With that, she walked out, closing Alanna's door behind her.

Alanna wondered if Miss Hauptmann ever smiled. It was rare for her to take such an instant dislike to anyone. She put on her white coat and sat down, scanning the referral list with interest. Most names were unfamiliar to her.

There was a computer terminal on the desk. She would have to find out what information she could access. No doubt someone would show her.

Taking her purse, she opened the door and set out to find the restrooms. When she returned to her office, a young woman was waiting for her.

"Doctor, the lady in room five is in labor."

Alanna entered the room to see a young Hispanic woman breathing heavily. Her blood pressure was 160/110. Her face and feet were swollen, and her reflexes were hyperactive. Alanna listened to the baby's heart and examined the woman. She was already four centimeters dilated.

"You're in labor, and your blood pressure is high. You need to go to the hospital right away. Who is your obstetrician?"

The woman shrugged and looked at her husband.

"She no speak English too good," he said, pulling a crumpled piece of paper from his pocket.

Alanna examined it. The woman was a County clinic patient. She was supposed to deliver at a hospital downtown, but Alanna doubted she'd make it.

"This is too far. You need to take her to the nearest hospital emergency room now. I'll give you directions. Do you understand?"

He nodded.

"Do you have a car?"

"We came on the bus."

Alanna turned to the nurse. "I can't let her take a bus. We'll need to call an ambulance. She's got severe toxemia, and she's not stable."

"I'm not allowed to call an ambulance."

"Then call the paramedics. Do it now," Alanna said, "before she has a seizure."

Alanna started an I.V. while she was waiting for the paramedics to arrive. When they came, she asked them to administer a dose of Magnesium Sulfate to stabilize the woman's pressure and to prevent seizures.

As the medics wheeled a gurney into the examination room, the woman screamed, and her face turned red with effort. Alanna grabbed a rubber glove and examined her.

"It's too late. We'll have to deliver her here."

She put on a pair of sterile gloves. The baby was crowning.

"Mucho dolor," the woman screamed. "Mucho."

The paramedic grinned at Alanna. "Better here than in the ambulance. Need a hand?"

"I'm worried she might seize. If you've got emergency airway equipment in that ambulance, please get it. I could use some Pitocin and some Lidocaine as well for after the delivery."

"You got it." The paramedic left the room just as the nurse arrived with the supplies.

Alanna eased the baby's head out, followed by a shoulder. The remainder of the baby slid out smoothly. Clamping the cord, she held him up for his mother.

"A boy. Congratulations."

The mother stopped screaming and looked with evident relief at her infant. Alanna dried the baby and placed him in his mother's arms. Her clothes and lab coat were covered in blood and amniotic fluid. There was a sudden large gush of blood, and Alanna pulled gently on the umbilical cord. The placenta came out into the steel basin.

Alanna massaged the uterus until it felt firm. She wiped

the blood and looked for lacerations. Everything seemed intact.

"Let's get a BP."

The girl struggled with the blood pressure cuff, applying it awkwardly and inflating it several times.

"I can't get it."

Alanna stripped her gloves, reapplied the cuff, and grabbed the stethoscope.

It was 140/100, not great, but better.

"Let's get her cleaned up, and the paramedics can transfer her to the nearest hospital. She'll need Magnesium Sulfate for at least twenty-four hours."

"You should probably get yourself cleaned up, Doc," the paramedic said. "Nice job."

The nurse took the blood pressure cuff from her and put it away. "We have scrubs and extra white coats in the hall closet next to the ladies' room."

Alanna stripped to her underwear, washed as best she could, and changed to clean scrubs. She rolled up her clothes and stuffed them in a plastic bag. The sneakers were probably unsalvageable. She'd add them to the collection she kept strictly for labor and delivery.

When she was done, she walked up to the nurse's station to write a note in the chart.

The chart was impressively organized. An extensive typed medical history was already in place.

"Do you know where the progress notes are kept?" Alanna asked a woman who was answering phones at the nurse's station.

"Oh, you don't need to write anything. All our charts are computerized. You can type out a note on your terminal, or if you don't have time, dictate into this. It'll be transcribed, put into the computer, and a hard copy printed for the chart." She handed Alanna a small Dictaphone.

"What about those histories?" Alanna asked. "How do you get them done so fast?"

The woman got up and motioned Alanna down the hall. She opened the door to a large room where about a dozen patients sat at computer terminals under the supervision of two clinic workers.

"It takes the patients about fifteen minutes to fill these out on the computer. It's all simple, yes, no questions. They can choose English or Spanish. Then the computer prints out a narrative for the chart. Most patients can be seen by our practitioners, but the computer selects those who need a doctor. Very efficient."

"I'll say. You have no idea what it's like reading a hospital chart written in completely indecipherable handwriting. I'm impressed."

Another young girl in white requested Alanna's presence down the hall, this time for a miscarriage. Over the next two hours, she admitted a probable acute appendicitis and a man with severe asthma. She saw several other patients who were not ill enough to be admitted but who required various minor surgical procedures ranging from biopsies to lancing a large abscess. When she finally looked up, it was ten o'clock and the waiting room was empty.

As she finished her last patient and was dictating her final note, Alanna realized what had nagged at her all evening. All the clinic personnel looked too young and sounded too uneducated to be handling the jobs they had.

Nurses who couldn't even manage to take a blood pressure reading made her uneasy. To be a nurse practitioner or physician assistant requires considerable training. Most of the clinic workers could barely speak English, and most looked like teenagers. She couldn't believe they were evaluating patients.

She pushed her hair back behind her ears and stood up slowly from the desk. She ached all over. She wanted to go home, take a warm bath, and an aspirin, and worry about this some other time. She walked down the hall and opened the door to her consultation room.

As she switched on the light, she realized she'd opened the wrong door. She started to close it when something caught her eye, causing her to look up and stare in shock. Standing next to an examination table was a complex machine of metal and wire with three jointed arms. It was hauntingly familiar.

"What are you doing in here?'

Alanna jumped as Miss Hauptmann came up behind her.

"Sorry, I was looking for my office. What is that?"

"It's a photographic machine. For research only. You won't need it." She gripped Alanna's shoulder and steered her firmly out of the room, shutting the light and closing the door behind her.

"Your room is here, doctor." She pointed to the adjacent door.

"Thank you." Alanna took her purse and searched for the car keys. Almost everyone was gone. Miss Hauptmann escorted her to the back door and locked it behind her.

The woman couldn't wait to be rid of her. There had to be a way to get a better look at that instrument. She knew she hadn't imagined it. It was familiar. Next time she came to Health Web, she would find a way into that room.

32

January 23, 1996, 1:45 p.m.
Los Angeles, California

B RIAN DREW, CEO OF HEALTH WEB, WAS IN A foul mood. Not only had his flight from Dallas to San Jose been delayed, but the airport traffic had reduced the speed of his limousine to a slow crawl. Now, his carefully planned afternoon schedule of meetings would have to be rearranged.

His driver stopped the car in front of the main entrance to ARI.

Drew retrieved his briefcase and stepped out. "Be back here in an hour."

ARI stood for American Robotics Institute, and until a few years ago, it had specialized in computer systems for controlling robots used in manufacturing car parts. Thanks to an infusion of venture capital and technical expertise, the company had changed direction and veered into the rapidly growing field of healthcare.

Howard Hauptmann, the company CEO, had promised him an impressive demonstration. Drew expected to be impressed, after all the money he had invested.

Hauptmann came to the lobby to greet him, and the two men went to the laboratory where Drew seated himself at the computer console. He clicked on the icon and was rewarded with soft music and a calm, friendly male voice.

"Hello there. I'm Dr. John, your guide to our diagnostic computer and health care team. Even if you've never used a computer before, you can follow my step-by-step instructions."

The system proceeded to take a detailed past medical history in which Drew was required to give all his illnesses, surgeries, family history, and medications, plus a detailed list of his current symptoms.

When he finished, Dr. John came on screen again. "It's time for your examination. Please follow the nurse into the next room."

"You'll have to settle for me, I'm afraid, sir," the project manager told him. "We don't have a nurse."

Drew and Hauptmann followed him next door to the robotics room, and Drew seated himself on an examination table. The robot, with its three flexible arms, stood by the examination table.

"This robot has a camera arm, a sound processing arm, and a touch sensor. All three robotic arms can work simultaneously, so an entire physical exam can be completed in under five minutes. Most physicians can't look in someone's eyes, feel their belly, and listen to their heart simultaneously. The robot can come up with a diagnosis and a management plan while ordering as few laboratory and imaging tests as possible."

"Does the patient ever get to see a human being?"

"That depends on how sick he is or how many expensive tests the computer thinks are needed. If a patient exceeds a certain expense threshold or has to be admitted to a hospital, he sees a physician first. We figure fewer than one in twenty patients will need to be seen. One of these computer robots can process one patient in about ten minutes.

"In a big clinic, one physician could have ten or twelve robotic exam rooms with a low-paid technician to guide the patients from place to place. One doctor could process three or four hundred patients a day while seeing fewer than twenty. If you think about the savings, they're enormous. No matter how high we price this system, if it eliminates fifteen doctors' salaries for everyone it needs, it'll pay for itself in no time."

Drew smiled for the first time that morning. He loved technology, and few things were more satisfying than contemplating the huge profit he could make from the healthcare system with this device. He'd placed one in a Health Web clinic recently and was anxious to find out how well it was working.

There had been a time when Drew had envisioned himself as a physician. He had gone to medical school, but as he worked through his clinical rotations, it became clear that hands-on doctoring was not for him.

He detested the blood, the pus, and the putrid odor of sick humanity. He had no patience for listening to the endless complaints of the ill and was revolted by their sweating, filthy bodies. In short, he was on his way to becoming a doctor who couldn't stand his patients.

He looked at his fellow students working hundred-hour weeks and suffering from severe sleep deprivation, and couldn't understand why anyone would put up with this for a lifetime.

It was at that moment that Drew envisioned his future. He would become rich and powerful by exploiting the labor of doctors instead of becoming one. Thus far, as CEO of Health Web, he had succeeded brilliantly, and Dr. John would be his crowning achievement.

33

January 24, 1996, 9:45 p.m.
Los Angeles, California

THE DEATH OF SUZANNE SAUNDERS PROVED unfortunate to everyone except Brian Drew. He sat savoring his second single malt scotch from the minibar in his suite. The odds of his acquisition had now changed dramatically in his favor. This had been a most satisfying trip; the death of an opposing board member and the ability to indulge himself in some discreet recreation that was so easily available in Los Angeles. Tomorrow, he would pay his respects to Colin Lancaster and assure himself that he did indeed have another vote on the Memorial Board of Directors.

His first act after the purchase was completed would be to fire Sherman Magnussen as chairman of the OB-GYN department and to ensure that no one else hired him. He'd been waiting for the opportunity since his undergraduate days at Princeton.

Magnussen, as a college senior, had been everything the young Drew aspired to. His dramatic looks, sharp cheekbones, ice-blue eyes, and tousled blond hair, combined with his wealth and social standing, had attracted a large crew of hangers-on.

Sadly, Drew's admiration had not been reciprocated. Magnussen had rejected Drew's attempts to join his circle and humiliated him in painfully embarrassing ways. He'd never forgotten his white-hot desire for revenge.

Drew finished his Scotch and considered his plans for the rest of his evening. The dark underbelly of Los Angeles offered so many tantalizing options.

34

———

January 25, 1996, 4:00 a.m.
Los Angeles, California

P ATROLLING THE STREETS OF LOS ANGELES near the notorious Ramona Gardens housing project was a job that demanded constant vigilance, even at four o'clock in the morning. The dead of night was the usual time for the various gangs that inhabited the project to consummate their drug deals or settle their scores with one another.

The two patrol officers in the Hollenbeck division squad car were alert for the sound of sudden gunfire as they cruised down Whittier Boulevard and explored the small dark side streets to the south bordering the intersection of the Pomona and Santa Ana freeways.

"Hey, what's that over there, under the freeway ramp?" the passenger said.

There was a shapeless bundle hidden in the shadows. It looked like a sleeping man. "Homeless. Probably drunk and passed out."

"Or dead?"

"Maybe. Let's check it out."

The two men got out of the patrol car, one holding a flashlight, and the other with his gun in hand. Together, they approached the man.

"Hey buddy, you okay?"

The stench hit them simultaneously. There was no mistaking the smell. He'd been dead for a while.

They moved closer and examined the body in the light. The dead man's clothes were filthy, but there was no sign of blood on them and no obvious sign of a gunshot or stab wound. The guy was young.

"Probably overdosed."

They went back to the car and radioed for the meat wagon. No point in a crime team. This didn't look like a crime, just another night at Ramona Gardens.

35

―――――

January 26, 1996, 8:00 a.m.
Los Angeles, California

"WHAT'VE YOU GOT FOR ME?" PATHOLOGIST Joseph Santiago put on a cover gown over his clothes and donned rubber gloves.

The County Morgue technician had prepared the body for autopsy and taken photographs, fingerprints, and dental x-rays. The body sent in by the Hollenbeck division the previous night had been easy to identify.

"His name is Jesus Morales. He's got a long record for drug dealing. He's supposed to be out on parole. I noticed something weird when I was undressing him. Take a look."

The technician slid out the refrigerator tray containing Morales' body and drew back the sheet. The body was covered in tattoos, tears on his cheek, a snake winding around one arm, and letters on the knuckles of both hands. His shaven head had the initials JM in an elaborate font and the symbol of an El Salvadoran gang. There was also a recent midline surgical scar dividing the belly and stitched up with an amateurish row of purple sutures.

Santiago raised his eyebrows. "Not very even are they? Looks like someone was letting a medical student practice." He probed the wound edges gently with a gloved finger. The tissue was soft, well past the point of rigor mortis. "Why don't you have someone call the County hospital and see if there's a record of his admission?"

The County had no record of Jesus Morales, nor did any other hospital within a twenty-mile radius of where he was found. Santiago ordered Morales transferred to a morgue table, where he opened him up to determine what kind of surgery he had undergone. When he was finished, he called the Robbery Homicide Division at Parker Center and asked for the homicide detective on call.

"It's Murray Mosher," the watch commander told him.

"Tell Murray to come down to the morgue as soon as he can make it. We've got a wacko on the loose."

36

———————

January 26, 1996, 730 a.m.
Los Angeles, California

THE CALL CAME JUST AS MURRAY MOSHER WAS preparing breakfast in the kitchen of his Pasadena bungalow. While his omelet cooked, he toasted a slice of French bread and brought the Los Angeles Times in from the front porch.

"Mosher here." He held the phone with one hand and used the other to slide his omelet onto a plate. He sampled it as he listened.

"I'll be there as soon as I can." Santiago had something interesting to show him, but Murray figured it could wait till after breakfast. After all, the guy was already dead. Murray brought his food to the table, put on a pair of wire-rimmed reading glasses, and scanned the headlines.

He was a wiry man, with thick brown hair and a mustache turning to gray, the hair beginning to recede at the crown. His face was long and craggy, with high cheekbones and a prominent nose, well-suited for supporting the glasses. Behind his back, they called him 'The Professor.' He supposed there were less flattering nicknames.

He abandoned the depressing headlines and turned his attention to the shelves that lined the small breakfast room. They were stacked with orderly piles of audio tapes, Murray's prize collection of old radio shows. Murray's mother was convinced that his passion for old detective shows led to his present career.

Unfortunately, as Murray had discovered, police detective work did not normally require much intellectual acumen. Most of it was either gang or domestic violence and lacked subtlety in either method or motive.

He finally settled on a 1945 rendition of Basil Rathbone as Sherlock Holmes to keep him entertained on his drive to the morgue. With a sigh, he put his dishes in the sink and strapped on his shoulder holster. It was time for him to head downtown and see what Santiago wanted.

Mosher arrived half an hour later, and Santiago pointed out the salient features of the refrigerated corpse.

"Someone's taken out his appendix, removed most of his small bowel, and sewed the remaining two ends together, here." Santiago held up a section of bowel, sloppily put together with purple thread. Murray stepped back and hoped his omelet would stay where it belonged.

"He's also missing his transverse colon. We found it stapled at both ends and stuffed into his pelvis. This reminds me of the kind of thing we used to do in pig lab when we were training, only in this case, Morales was the pig. We should call this killer The Surgeon."

"You think we got a doctor here?"

Santiago shook his head. "Not necessarily. Whoever did this has access to surgical equipment, but his technique is lousy. If it's a doctor, it's an internist. No experienced surgeon would tie knots like that."

"Maybe we can identify the company that manufactured the suture and staples. I'll get the lab boys on it."

"You'd better. I got a bad feeling we'll run across this guy again."

37

January 27, 1996, 12:30 a.m.
Los Angeles, California

THE HOMELESS GUY TOOK THE FINAL SWIG OUT of his half-pint bottle of cheap whiskey, tossed it into the gutter and listened to the satisfying clink of broken glass as it hit the curb. Swaying erratically on his feet, he lurched south on Alameda, heading toward his favorite sleeping place, a cozy underpass of the Santa Monica Freeway. His sanctuary was protected from wind and rain in the winter and provided a shady refuge from the hot sun in the summer. In addition, it was far away from any of the other homeless, so he could sleep easy, unworried that he might be attacked during the night and robbed of his few remaining possessions.

Tomorrow, though, he'd have to sleep in one of those shelters. He'd spent the last of his money on whiskey and had to start panhandling again. No one would give him anything, looking and smelling like this.

Alameda was deserted this time of night. The avenue didn't lead anywhere anyone would want to go after midnight. A dark van cruised slowly down the street behind him and pulled to a stop a few yards ahead.

The passenger door opened, and a man got out and walked toward him. From the way he walked, he was probably a fag, but the homeless guy wasn't worried much. No one propositioned him once they got close enough.

"Hey, mister."

He stopped weaving down the street and looked up. He could see the figure clearly in the glare of the streetlight. He was a Black boy, thin and frail-looking with thick, pouty lips smeared with lipstick.

"Wanna earn a quick twenty?" The boy reached into his jeans pocket, waving a bill.

The homeless man's eyes followed the cash. The guy was half his size. He could jerk him off in two minutes and break him in two if he tried anything funny. He lurched toward the money.

The boy backed off in the direction of the van.

"In here. I don't do nothin' in the street."

He shrugged and followed him. The boy opened the back doors and motioned for him to climb in, standing aside as he stepped up to the padded bottom.

"Gimme the money first," he said as he settled himself on the floor.

The boy handed him the bill.

"There's another one for after."

As the homeless man turned to tuck the twenty away, he heard the clang of the back door closing and the sudden acceleration of the van's engine. That fucker had locked him inside! It was pitch black, and he realized the back of the van had no windows and was cut off from the front compartment. He had no idea where they were taking him, or why, but he suddenly had a bad feeling about it.

38

January 28, 1996, 10:30 p.m.
Los Angeles, California

I T HAD BEEN AN EXCEPTIONALLY SLOW NIGHT on Sunset
Boulevard, and the hooker was ready to call it quits for
the evening. All she'd scored in the five hours she'd been
parading along her stretch of Sunset had been ten bucks for
a quick blow job in a convenient back alley.

The two girls who worked the other side of the street
had been picked up by a couple of guys in a white BMW
over an hour ago and hadn't returned. Most of the night's
foot traffic had subsided, and if she hadn't been afraid that
her pimp would accuse her of holding out on him, she'd
have split half an hour ago.

She took out a mirror from her sequinned shoulder bag
and reapplied bright red lipstick over her generous mouth.
She ran her tongue over her new bridge, a business expense
paid for by her pimp after he'd knocked out her front teeth
in a fit of temper over her decreasing revenues.

She patted her braided hair extensions, sucked in her

stomach, and straightened the black stockings she wore with her high-heeled pumps. She began to walk the street again, closer to the curb, looking hopefully at any car that slowed even slightly at the sight of her thin waist and generous ass in the tight black miniskirt.

A dark van pulled up beside her, and the passenger window rolled down.

"How much?"

"Fifty."

"Get in."

"I got a place around the corner."

She heard the door click as the window glass closed, and she stepped off the curb. The car door opened, and she got her first good look at the driver. He was big and pockmarked with a thin mustache. Something about him gave her a bad feeling, and she hesitated.

"I don't have all night."

Leaning over, he gripped her arm and pulled her into the passenger's seat. He reached past her and slammed the door. The car lurched, taking off down the boulevard.

"Right turn," she said.

The guy ignored her. Shit. All she needed was some John who was gonna rough her up and make it impossible for her to work for weeks. Or even worse. The knot in the pit of her stomach tightened painfully.

As he sped past her corner, she looked in the rearview mirror. A second guy emerged from behind her seat. As the car slowed for a red light, she tried to make a break for it, but the driver grabbed her arm with a grip like steel. From behind, she felt her head being pulled back. A wet cloth with a strange smell covered her nose and mouth, and then, nothing.

39

____

January 29, 7:10 a.m., 1996
Los Angeles, California

Slipping on a protective cloth gown and mask, Murray Mosher entered the double doors of the morgue. It was a good thing he hadn't had a chance to have breakfast yet. The scent of formalin always made him feel like he was going to upchuck, even though he'd become hardened over the years to some of the more revolting smells associated with dead bodies. He never understood how those ghouls in the county pathology department could spend their days cutting up stiffs for a living.

Santiago had awakened him from a fretful sleep less than an hour ago.

"You'd better come in here, Murray. I think we got two more last night."

"Two more what?"

"Dead patients of The Surgeon."

Murray had dragged himself out of bed, run a comb through his thinning hair, cut himself shaving, and put on his grungiest jeans. Everything he wore today would need deodorizing.

When the first body was brought in, Mosher immediately recognized the style of the surgical incision with its awkward purple sutures. This time, it divided the chest wall.

The color of the heart was almost black, as if there had been a massive heart attack. Santiago severed the heart from the four major vessels that anchored it in the chest and placed it in a tray under the light so that he could examine it more carefully.

"Jesus. This heart's missing all its coronary arteries," he said.

"Any ID?" Mosher asked.

"Yeah. The fingerprints match a downtown panhandler. He was arrested several times for drunk and disorderly behavior."

"Who found him?"

"An anonymous caller. He was under the Alameda Street off-ramp to the Santa Monica Freeway. The other body's over there," Santiago said, gesturing across the morgue.

"Shit. This is the third one in five days. What'd he do to him?"

"Her, Murray. It's her, and she's missing her gallbladder. Come take a look."

The second body on the mortuary slab was a black woman, probably in her early twenties, with generous breasts and hips and shapely thighs. A face that, except for its missing teeth, had been pretty. Her surgical scar was a large curve on her upper right abdomen.

"How come I wasn't called when they found them?" Murray said. "The Surgeon is my case!"

"The calls went to the Rampart division. I didn't realize

until both of them were assigned to me this morning that it was the same killer. We have a serial here. The homicide detectives working the cases will give you all they've got."

"We know who she is?"

"Yeah, a hooker who works Sunset Boulevard. They found her this morning near the Silver Lake exit. She died lying on her back. All the postmortem lividity is on her shoulders and buttocks. She was strapped down, arms and legs. The measurements of the strap marks are identical to the other two bodies. They found her dressed and lying on her stomach, so she was transported and dumped after death."

"Anything else I should know?" Mosher asked.

"His technique's getting better. The knots are more evenly tied where he closed the incision, and he didn't damage the common bile duct. This girl didn't bleed to death. If he'd taken the trouble to wake her, or breathe for her, she'd have lived through the experience."

"What'd she die from?"

"I won't know until I process the slides, but I bet he turned off the ventilator while her diaphragm was paralyzed by the anesthetic. He has been anesthetizing all his victims. We've found traces of the anesthetic agents on the mass spectrograph."

"Any evidence of rape?"

"No one left any sperm in her, rape or otherwise. Either she had a slow night, or she made her Johns use condoms. Wonder why the killer went all the way to Hollywood."

"The easiest way to pick up a lone woman if you want to operate on one. The homeless ones downtown usually aren't loners. It's too dangerous. Has the media gotten wind of this yet?"

"Remarkably, no. Of course, most reporters aren't all that

interested in dead homeless people and hookers. But one of these days this bastard is going to kill some ordinary citizen and you're going to have headlines from here to Asuza."

"Don't remind me. I hate all those nosy reporters."

"Well, I hope you solve this before they get hold of it," Santiago said, "or they'll crucify you. You know how they get when someone withholds a good story."

"I'll get this fucker," Murray said as he headed out of the morgue and back to his car to call the Ramparts division. "One of these days, there is gonna be a witness."

40

January 29, 1996, 7:25 a.m.
Los Angeles, California

LISA KEATING LEANED OVER AND RETCHED INTO the toilet in the ladies' locker room. She couldn't seem to stop vomiting even though her stomach was empty. It couldn't have been anything she'd eaten. She'd awakened feeling completely out of sorts and had decided to skip breakfast.

She flushed the toilet and washed out her mouth at the sink. She looked awful. There were huge dark rings under her eyes, and her hair was damp with sweat. She was probably coming down with some virus. She'd lie down in one of the on-call rooms and tell Sherman she was going home for the rest of the day. He wouldn't mind. God, he was revolting. The garbage a girl had to sleep with to get ahead these days.

She stripped off her sweat-soaked shirt and reached for a new one. Her breasts felt sore and heavy, premenstrual, and her lower belly cramped slightly. Maybe she'd better put in a tampon. She'd probably lost track of the days. She retrieved her purse from her locker and checked her appointment book. It had been thirty-one days since she last menstruated, and she usually bled on day 28. Stress, most likely. She couldn't be pregnant.

The thought haunted her as she left the locker room and chose one of the more remote on-call rooms to lie down in. She couldn't be. She'd used her diaphragm every time with a double dose of jelly. Finally, unable to sleep, she left the room and headed for the satellite lab adjacent to Labor and Delivery.

She slipped a specimen bottle, a urine pregnancy test, and the appropriate chemicals into the pocket of her white lab coat and left before she ran into Gabrielle Broder. She wouldn't believe Lisa was ill. She was jealous of her, just like all the other residents.

None of them appreciated her unique and innovative ideas. They expected her to waste her time doing grunt work like they did. They all resented her special relationship with the chairman.

Not that Sherman understood her either. He was just hot for her body, but he was willing to pay the price. He freed up her time so she could devote it to caring for his high-profile patients.

Lisa returned to the on-call room, locked the door, and collected her urine in the privacy of the bathroom. When the disc developed a blue plus sign, she was astonished. An unplanned pregnancy only occurs when you are too stupid to use protection. The thought of carrying Sherman Magnussen's fetus made her want to puke all over again.

Oh well, she was sure he'd pay for the abortion. The question was, where to have it? She'd have to go out of town somewhere. The last thing she needed was to be the subject of hospital gossip.

On the other hand, perhaps she was being too hasty. It

was possible that being the potential mother of Magnussen's brat could be worth a great deal more than a paid-up abortionist's bill. She would have to give the situation careful thought. Perhaps there was a way this unfortunate accident could be turned to her advantage.

41

―――――

January 29, 1996, 9:15 a.m.
Los Angeles, California

THINGS WERE GOING FROM BAD TO WORSE. Sherman Magnussen told his secretary to hold his calls and slammed his office door.

First, the Lancaster woman and her untimely demise just as she had successfully produced the long-awaited Lancaster heir. Then, Martin Lancaster announced that he was withdrawing his financial support for Magnusen's pet project. If the hospital sold out to Health Web, Magnussen could kiss the plans for his new fertility center goodbye.

The final straw arrived this morning in the form of a certified letter from Martin Lancaster's attorneys. Lancaster was suing the hospital, the Obstetrics and Gynecology department, Vincent Swerdlow, and all the physicians and nurses involved in his wife's care for gross negligence.

The buzzer sounded on his phone.

"I thought I told you not to disturb me."

"I'm sorry, doctor," his secretary said, "but Dr. Keating is here. She says it's urgent."

"Send her in."

Lisa stepped into the office and locked the door as usual. Magnusen thought she looked unwell. Her usually rosy complexion was sallow, and there were circles under her eyes. She hadn't taken the trouble to put on her make-up for him. Lisa was upset about something.

"What's wrong?" he asked, leaning back in his chair and clasping his hands behind his head.

"I'm pregnant, and it's yours. There's no other possibility."

"I see. And you'd like me to pay for the abortion?"

"Is that what you want me to do? Abort your child?"

"Lisa, be an adult, for God's sake. You had an accident. Unless you're interested in being a single mother, I don't see a better alternative. Do you?"

"You could divorce Annabelle, and we could get married."

"If I divorce Annabelle, she'll take me for every penny I have, and you'll be living with me in a studio apartment in Culver City."

"You know you're exaggerating. You don't care about me at all, do you? I'm just a convenient fuck."

Magnussen got up from his desk and pulled her to him, patting her head awkwardly into his shoulder.

"You know that's not true, honey. I'm crazy about you. I'm just not prepared to be a parent again."

Actually, it was true, but he needed to calm her down. The last thing he wanted was a divorce from Annabelle. She was the one with the money, the one whose family fortune had purchased the ten thousand square foot home in Bel Air and the twin Bentleys. She was the one who paid for the boys' tuition at Stanford and at USC Law School. His salary as department chairman was petty cash compared to what Annabelle provided, and over the years, he'd gotten used to the lifestyle.

The fact that Annabelle made love like a dead lizard was a minor inconvenience when you considered how brilliantly she performed as a hostess. He'd made a mistake with Lisa. Most of his dalliances had been one-night stands at out-of-town medical meetings or wives of fellow physicians who had as much to lose as he did if they were discovered. He'd never fucked a resident before, and he swore to himself that he never would again.

Lisa pushed herself away and stared at him. He was expecting to see tears, a trembling mouth, perhaps, or one of those seductive poses she was so good at. Instead, her stare was ice cold and full of frightening determination.

"If you don't tell her, I will. I will not be used and made a fool of. We can do this discreetly, or we can ruin your reputation as well as your marriage. It's up to you."

42

January 30, 1996, 1:00 p.m.
Los Angeles, California

THE MAGNUSSEN ESTATE WAS A SUBSTANTIAL English Tudor home, tucked into a cul-de-sac in lower Bel Air. Lisa pulled her car into the circular driveway, smoothed the skirt on her Donna Karan suit, and rang the front doorbell.

A maid in a pink uniform answered the door.

"I'm Dr. Keating. I'm a friend of Dr. Magnussen's. Would you ask Mrs. Magnussen if she has a few moments to talk with me?" Lisa rehearsed this opening line, with variations, on her drive up.

The maid asked her to wait in the entryway and disappeared toward the back of the house. Lisa glanced with approval at the shining parquet floors, the fresh flowers, and the expensive artwork in the vestibule, and took a quick look through an archway into the main living room. The room was huge, with dark wood beams, oriental rugs, sofas upholstered in chintz, and expensive antiques. No wonder Sherman wasn't anxious to leave his wife.

The maid reappeared and motioned for Lisa to follow.

Annabelle Magnussen was sitting on her back patio, finishing a light lunch of stuffed papaya salad and a glass of Chablis. She turned as Lisa approached and gestured for her to take the chair opposite.

"Have a seat. Would you like a glass of wine?"

Annabelle was in her forties with tight skin and perfect features. Her blonde hair was artfully streaked, and her face flawlessly made-up. She was wearing spandex tights and a leotard with the logo of the most prestigious gym in Beverly Hills. All things considered, she was precisely what Lisa had expected, a perfect foil for Sherman.

Lisa sat down, crossed her legs, and refused the drink.

"I don't want to waste your time, Mrs. Magnussen, so I'll come directly to the point. I'm pregnant, courtesy of your husband. He'll be asking you for a divorce shortly. He appeared to be having difficulty breaking the news to you himself, so I thought I'd better. I hope there won't be too much unpleasantness. I'm sure we'd both prefer to handle this in a civilized manner." She stared, without blinking, at Annabelle, waiting for her reaction.

Annabelle put down her Chablis. The corners of her mouth turned up in a smile which blossomed into a hearty laugh. "Oh, you poor thing. I didn't think girls were still that naive. Sherman will never divorce me. He likes my money too much. Do you think you're the first of his little playthings?"

Lisa flushed. "Perhaps he was careful not to impregnate the others."

Annabelle leaned forward and returned Lisa's stare. "Let us understand one another. Sherman fools around because

I let him, and I let him because it suits me. If you were expecting an outraged, mortified wife who would immediately call her lawyer and institute divorce proceedings, I'm sorry to disappoint you.

"You screwed around and you got caught. Given your profession, I'm sure you know what to do about it. I assure you, your devastating revelation will not gain you a husband or any large sum of money. I would suggest you leave now." She rang a silver bell that sat on the patio table. "Maria will show you out."

Lisa didn't wait for Maria. She pushed back the chair, stalked across the patio, and slammed the Magnussens' front door. She floored her gas pedal as her car screeched out of their driveway.

What a bitch. Annabelle wasn't at all what Lisa had expected. Not that Lisa wanted to marry Sherman. She would be quite adequately compensated if she made his life miserable. But there had to be other ways to do that. Perhaps she needed to rethink her strategy.

43

January 31, 1996, 5:30 p.m.
Los Angeles, California

THE SMELL OF BLOOD IN THE DELIVERY ROOM was making Lisa Keating nauseous again. She had finished sewing an episiotomy on one of her clinic patients and contemplated her next move. How, she wondered, did women put up with being pregnant if all they did was puke all the time? It was truly remarkable that we managed to sustain the population.

She had underestimated Annabelle Magnussen. She had assumed Annabelle would be one of those compliant doctors' wives. Lisa had no idea that Annabelle was, in fact, the true power in the Magnussen family. What a shame she didn't want to divorce Sherman. It would have been a nice touch.

There was something about Annabelle that reminded Lisa of her mother, although Lisa's mother had acquired her wealth by marrying rather than inheriting. She'd taught Lisa, early on, that the only way you got respect was by having lots of money and the trappings that went with it. It didn't matter who you had to use or what you had to do to obtain it.

Lisa's mother, for example, had amassed quite a tidy sum by marrying a series of stepfathers, none of whom could keep their hands to themselves. It hadn't taken long for Lisa to figure out that two could play the same game. Her mother's husbands had supplied their nubile, teenage step-daughter with a Mercedes convertible, expensive jewelry, and a large bank account. If she played her cards right, this most recent one would finance her when she opened her Beverly Hills private practice.

In addition, Lisa had discovered she had skills that tran-scended the merely sexual. It wouldn't be long before she became an exceptionally wealthy, famous, and powerful woman.

Lisa signed out the Labor and Delivery board to the night on-call team and retreated to the locker room to change. The Donna Karan would have to do. She didn't have time to go home and change before her appointment. She buttoned the collar of her crisp white blouse, combed her hair neatly, and reduced her make-up to a touch of blush and some pale lipstick. Glamour Girl was not the image she wanted to create. Today's role was the innocent victim.

The law offices of Geneva Jenson were in Beverly Hills, on North Camden Drive. Ms. Jenson didn't usually see clients after five, but she made an exception when Lisa had explained her predicament and schedule. There was no question in Lisa's mind that Geneva was the attorney she wanted. Geneva had handled and won any number of high-profile sex discrimination and sexual harassment cases over the past several years. She was the darling of the feminist groups. If Lisa could convince her to take the case, she would have an excellent chance of winning a large sum from the hospital and Magnussen.

Geneva Jenson was in her fifties. Her tall, slim figure was dressed in a conservative navy-blue suit. Thick, dark hair, cut in a short, geometric bob, flattered her strong face, covered with large maroon-framed glasses. Her smile was warm as she ushered Lisa into her office.

Lisa smiled and sat facing her, hands folded demurely on her lap. "Where would you like me to begin?"

"You mentioned sexual harassment over the telephone?"

"It's more complicated than that. It's sexual harassment, rape, and I'm pregnant. I'm a resident in the OB-GYN department at Los Angeles Memorial. The man responsible is my chairman, Sherman Magnussen."

"How long has he been harassing you?"

"For months, but I didn't know how to label it then. He was careful about it. At the beginning, it was just verbal flirting and sexual innuendos, never when anyone else was in earshot. Then he started calling me into his office for 'conferences.'

"He'd show me into the room and run his hand over my buttocks, or accidentally touch my breasts. It made me uncomfortable, but I was afraid to offend him. He was my chairman, and my residency was literally in his hands. He implied that if I were cooperative, he could help launch my medical career.

"I tried to avoid him, but it's hard to say no when the chairman tells you to show up in his office. Anyway, a few weeks ago, I went to the department office to pick up my mail. Everyone was gone for the day, and I thought he was too.

"Just as I was leaving, he came out of his office. He asked me to step in and talk to him for a moment. When I did, he locked the door behind us and grabbed me. I tried to scream, but there wasn't anyone within earshot. He just threw me on the floor and raped me. Afterwards, he said he'd wanted to fuck me ever since I was an intern, and that if I was a good girl, kept my mouth shut, and visited him regularly after hours, he'd make it worth my while."

Geneva was writing notes on a yellow pad of legal paper. She paused and pushed her glasses up on her nose with her pen. "What did you say?"

"I didn't say anything. I was too upset. I just straightened my clothes and asked if I could go now. He unlocked the door and held it open for me. I went home and took a long, hot bath."

"Did he assault you sexually again?"

"I didn't give him the opportunity. I managed to avoid him for a few weeks, but then I missed my period."

"Had you done anything to prevent a possible pregnancy, such as a morning-after pill?"

Lisa shook her head. "The rape happened three weeks after my previous period. I assumed I'd ovulated already and didn't need to worry, but I must have been late that cycle. When I didn't bleed for the next two weeks, I did a pregnancy test."

"What made you decide to sue for sexual harassment, doctor? Was it learning you were pregnant?"

Lisa nodded. Then she began to cry. "I told him. I don't know what I expected. Maybe an apology, or an offer to pay my expenses for an abortion, or maybe just a little human kindness, but I didn't get it. He was such an arrogant bastard. I finally decided to stop acting like a victim and fight back." She fumbled in her purse for a Kleenex and wiped away the tears. Then she looked up at Geneva. "Can you help me?"

"I can try. The first thing I need to ask is what you plan to do about the pregnancy."

"I'd like to get rid of it as soon as possible. It makes me feel unclean."

"You must make sure that the tissue is saved for genetic studies so that we have evidence available should Dr. Magnussen try to deny paternity. Do you have any witnesses, or know of any other women residents who may have shared your chairman's unwanted attentions?"

"I don't know if he's ever tried it with anyone else. No one's ever said. I'm certain no one witnessed his behavior toward me. As I said, he was careful."

Geneva smiled at her. "Men who behave this way usually have a history. It's just a question of approaching people and asking the right questions. Once women find they're not alone, you'd be surprised how many fellow victims and supporters you might have.

"I'll need a list from you of other women residents, nurses, secretaries, anyone in his orbit. Past residents would be useful because they have much less to lose, especially if they no longer practice at Memorial. At the moment, you realize, it's just your word against his."

"Will you take my case?"

"I'd like to, provided we can obtain enough evidence to file suit. I'm a great fan of women in medicine, and I admire your courage in coming forward. It disgusts me that the head of Women's Health, at the most prestigious hospital in Los Angeles could behave this way. You're doing a service to other women."

Lisa favored Geneva with one of her more charming smiles. Things were working out splendidly. Now all she had to do was rid herself of this troublesome fetus.

January 31, 1996, 6:45 p.m.
Los Angeles, California

BRIAN DREW SAT BACK IN HIS LEATHER CHAIR and listened to the voice at the other end of the phone.

"You've exceeded my expectations. I couldn't be more pleased." He listened for a moment longer, then nodded. "I do think your performance deserves an extra reward. Shall we say another ten thousand?"

Drew hung up the telephone and toyed with a gold Mont Blanc fountain pen, weighing his options. He had never anticipated that Lisa Keating would be so creative when he'd recruited her during her internship. At the time, all he'd had in mind was a set of eyes and ears in Los Angeles Memorial. He paid Lisa to report to him and, if possible, to find a way to make Sherman Magnussen's life miserable. Well, she had certainly done that. And far more. It was a pleasure to find an underling almost as ruthless as he was. Lisa's latest move had given him a brilliant idea. Drew couldn't wait to see how it was going to turn out.

45

———

February 1,1996 8:45 a.m.
Los Angeles, California

MURRAY DROPPED A PILE OF PAPERS ONTO HIS desk and settled himself into his chair.

With a sigh, he got to work, reviewing the folders on the three victims of The Surgeon.

He'd returned from the Ramparts division with his first piece of solid information. The killer had gotten careless. This time, there was a witness, a fellow hooker who had noticed her colleague getting into a dark van driven by a Caucasian male. She hadn't seen the license plate. That was too much to hope for, but her curiosity had been aroused by the fact that the car hadn't made a right turn at the corner. Her friend always took her John to the room she rented around the corner.

There was fiber evidence this time as well, a few strands of burgundy carpet caught in the heel of her pumps. The lab had traced it to a brand of commercial carpeting used in the 1995 Dodge Caravan. This particular shade of burgundy was the interior for the black body. Unfortunately, large numbers of that popular make and model were sold in Los Angeles.

Murray had already obtained a printout of every owner within a twenty-mile radius of downtown. He'd get one of his team to start cross-checking the owners, looking for anyone with a record or employed by a hospital, surgery center, or medical supply house. It was a tedious job, and there was no guarantee that the car wasn't out of state or stolen.

Advanced Surgical Products, a huge company with worldwide distribution, manufactured the suture and staples. Murray checked with every hospital and surgery center in Los Angeles County. More than half obtained their supplies from Advanced Surgical. The large hospitals contracted directly with the company.

The smaller surgery centers and doctors' offices obtained their supplies from medical supply companies, which provided one-stop shopping for offices that weren't purchasing enough to qualify for volume discounts. Murray had a list of all of those as well. It was smaller than he expected due to all the big fish swallowing the little ones. There were only half a dozen firms left in Los Angeles. He chewed his pencil and sighed.

"Any luck?" His partner, Roger Roth, opened the office door and slammed it behind him. He was carrying a large computer printout and a brown paper grocery bag.

"I don't know where to start eliminating. This guy could be a doctor, a nurse, or any other kind of employee of a dozen hospitals, half a dozen medical supply houses, a hundred surgical centers, or any medical office that orders from those medical supply houses. There's got to be something else."

"I talked to Santiago this morning. He's got some more mass spectrograph results for you. All the victims had been given a drug called Ketamine. It's an anesthetic agent, but it's not used very commonly because it causes hallucinations. Mostly, they use it on animals."

Roth reached into his bag, pulled out a pastry, and offered the remainder of the bag to Murray, who helped himself.

"Great. So now we look at all the veterinarians and animal research labs in town."

Roth laughed. "This is going to make our job a lot easier. I called the company that manufactures the drug. It's not a big seller. They sell it directly to only two hospitals in town, L.A. Memorial and the big County hospital. Three medical supply houses distribute it. We should be able to get their customer list."

Murray bit into his pastry and screwed up his nose in distaste. "What is this?"

"Don't you like it?" Roth looked wounded. "It's fat-free and sugar-free. Much healthier for you than those doughnuts you're always eating."

"Yeah, sure." Not for the first time, Murray wondered why the brass had seen fit to pair him with a health food nut who put alfalfa sprouts on everything. He put the pastry down on his desktop.

"Why don't you head out to the hospitals? Try nursing administration. They should be able to tell you how much of the stuff was ordered, and they should be able to account for every vial. Hospitals usually keep track of that sort of thing. I'll see if I can get a customer and an employee list from the medical supply houses."

"Right."

"Oh, and Roth, I'd tell them I'm looking for a drug pusher, not a serial killer, okay."

"Murray," said Roth as he headed out the door, "do I look like I was born yesterday?"

Murray waited till his partner was out of sight before depositing the pastry in the trash.

46

February 1, 1996, 11:00 a.m.
Los Angeles, California

MOSHER PARKED HIS UNMARKED CAR IN FRONT of Health Web Medical Supply Corporation's main warehouse in the City of Commerce. The neighborhood was depressingly industrial with large commercial buildings alternating with garbage-strewn empty lots, crossed by railroad tracks. The warehouse was a two-story, dirty beige stucco building with iron gates guarding the ground-floor windows.

Mosher turned off his ignition, ejected a 1945 Sam Spade episode from his cassette player, and walked to the front door. A wiry black man in a security guard's uniform looked up from a desk.

"Can I help you?"

"I'm Dr. Mosher. I'm here to see the chief administrator."

"You got an appointment?"

"No, but I was in the area. I'm sure he'll see me. It's regarding a large account."

"One minute." The guard picked up a phone and spoke quietly into it. Then he nodded. Getting up, he handed Murray a visitor's badge and escorted him through a metal detector into an inner lobby.

"Second floor, to your left. Mr. Henderson's office."

"Thanks." Murray was glad he'd left his semi-automatic in the trunk of his car. Neither of the other two supply houses he'd visited had been quite so security-conscious. Of course, they'd been in somewhat better locations. One was in Burbank, the other in El Segundo.

The elevator creaked to a stop and let Murray out in a carpeted hallway. He turned left and knocked at a door that said Administration. He entered an air-conditioned anteroom decorated with an attractive secretary.

"Have a seat, doctor. Mr. Henderson's on the phone, but he'll be able to see you as soon as he gets off."

Henderson was a bull-necked man with a shaven head and neatly clipped gray mustache. He held out a beefy hand to Murray for a shake. "What can I do for you, doc?"

"It's lieutenant, actually," Murray said, exhibiting his badge. "I need your help, Mr. Henderson, and I thought Doctor would cause less talk among the employees."

Henderson drew away, a scowl on his face. "What's this about?"

"There's a new, dangerous street drug we've been encountering in the past few weeks called Ketamine. We're trying to trace the source and the pushers. Most likely, it's a rogue lab, but we wanted to check inventory with the legitimate dealers first. You may have an employee who's lifting it. I need a copy of all the orders you've had for the drug in the past year, as well as a complete list of all your employees."

"We've got nothing to hide, lieutenant. I'll have my secretary put it together for you." Henderson picked up his phone. "It'll be a few minutes."

"While we wait, I'd like to inventory your current stock."

"I'll call down and find out what we have," Henderson said.

"If you don't mind, I'd prefer to count myself."

Henderson shrugged. "Whatever you say. I'll go down there with you."

They took the elevator one floor down and through a set of double doors to a large open storage area where aisles of shelving contained cartons of medical equipment. Henderson took out a set of keys and opened a smaller room at the far end where the drugs were kept. An elderly man in a white lab coat glanced up from his desk.

"George, we got any Ketamine?"

"I think so, Mr. Henderson. It should be in that cabinet behind you."

Murray opened the cabinet door labeled K-M and removed the carton labeled Ketamine. There were twenty-four vials.

"That's the whole supply?"

"I believe so," George said. "We don't stock much. Don't get many orders for it."

"Thanks."

They returned to Henderson's office, where he handed Murray the printout.

"I appreciate your help," Murray said. "I'd keep this between us if you don't mind."

"I don't mind, but if one of my boys is stealing, I want to know about it."

"You bet." Murray held out his hand and shook Henderson's again. Then he headed to his car. He had a lot of data to review, and it would be a long day.

47

February 2, 1996, 4:10 a.m.
Los Angeles, California

MOSHER TOSSED FITFULLY IN A TROUBLED SLEEP until the phone rang. It was ten minutes past four in the morning. He rolled over, grabbed the receiver, and identified the voice of the night secretary at Parker Center.

"You're needed at a crime scene. We think it's another victim of The Surgeon."

"Where?" Murray flicked on his bedside lamp and sat up, swinging his feet over the side of the bed and reaching for a pen and paper on his bedside table to write down the address.

"They found a woman's nude body dumped under the San Bernardino Freeway near Brooklyn Avenue. Body's still warm."

"Who found it?"

"Some trucker. He got off at that exit and made a left when he noticed it. Called the cops from his car phone. The patrol officer who answered the call saw she had a surgical incision and asked me to get hold of you."

"I'm on my way," Murray said. "Call Santiago, will you? I'd like him there. And tell the crime team not to move the body till I get there."

By the time Murray arrived, there was quite a crowd of police cars. The patrol officers had placed barricades and yellow tape around a large area. The police photographer was waiting for the go-ahead. Everyone else stood behind the barrier and watched.

Murray walked over to the officer in charge. "Anyone touch the body?"

"I checked to be sure she didn't need an ambulance instead of a homicide detective, but I didn't move anything."

"What about the trucker?"

"He says he stayed in his truck and waited for the cops. He's over there. We told him to wait till we'd finished getting his statement."

Murray shone his flashlight on the ground to be sure he wasn't walking over any potential evidence and slipped under the crime scene tape. The victim appeared to be a young woman in her twenties. She was lying on her back, legs slightly parted, arms slack at her sides. She had short, dark hair and a voluptuous body. Her jaw was relaxed and open, her blue eyes wide and expressionless.

There was blood on her inner thighs and the dark bush of black hair between them. Her belly was marred by a six-inch-long bikini incision, closed with large purple stitches. Murray looked carefully at the upper arms and upper thighs. He could see the indentations of the straps that had held her immobile. It was The Surgeon again. Murray had no doubt.

The girl's hands were clean and well-groomed with

short nails and colorless polish. Her toes showed signs of a recent pedicure. The short hair was fashionably cut, and a small pair of diamond stud earrings was inserted into her earlobes. This was no homeless person, and he doubted she was a hooker.

He turned his head as Santiago arrived, kneeled beside her, and gently flexed her arm and jaw.

"No rigor at all," he said. "This girl probably died less than two hours ago. Any idea who she is?"

Murray shook his head. "I'll have Detective Headquarters Division check out all the missing person complaints against her description. We'll print her and run the prints through all the usual databases. Someone should be able to identify her."

Santiago was busy taking the body temperature and examining the incision. He rolled the body gently to the right.

"Died on her back, just like the others. Let's finish the photographs, get her in the wagon, and take her downtown. I want to get started on her autopsy."

Murray motioned to the photographer, who began to do his job as the patrol officers and the coroner's assistant brought over the body bag with which they would transfer the girl's remains.

"Okay, boys," Murray said. "Bag every scrap you can find and dust the area for tire and fingerprints."

He walked over to the ten-wheeler trailer truck parked across the street. The driver was smoking a cigarette and listening to a country western radio station. He turned off the radio as Murray approached.

"What time did you find her?"

The driver, a big, red-faced, white-haired man, looked at his watch. "About half past three, I think."

"Tell me about it."

The guy shrugged. "I was driving east. I got a delivery to make on Brooklyn Avenue, so I got off and started to turn left. I spotted the girl. I wouldn't have called the cops if she hadn't been stark naked. I see lots of homeless people sleeping under the freeways. But this scared me. "

"You see any cars get off before you? Any other people on foot?"

The driver shook his head. "Nah. It's dead as a graveyard at this hour. That's why I like to drive at night. No traffic."

"You get out of the car to see if the girl was hurt?"

"I figure I got involved enough calling the cops. It wasn't my business to get out of the truck."

"Let me see your license and registration, please."

He copied the man's name, address, and license number into his notebook. He'd check to see if the trucker had a record. He'd also make sure the men took his finger and shoe prints. It wasn't unusual for the good Samaritan who discovers the body to turn out to be the killer.

"I'd like you to come downtown this morning and give us a formal statement," he said. "I'll have one of the officers escort you."

"No problem." The driver put out his cigarette. "I hope you catch the bastard."

Murray put away his notebook and headed back to his car. He wondered again who the girl was.

48

———

February 2, 1996, 6:00 a.m.
Los Angeles, California

S HE DREAMT SHE WAS IN THE HOSPITAL, trapped in her
bed and attached to I.V. lines everywhere. Strange
nurses with hideous faces were injecting her with lethal
drugs. No matter which way she turned to escape, someone
grabbed her and subdued her with a hypo spray. Alanna
awoke with her heart pounding and every joint in her body
screaming in pain.

She must be coming down with the flu. She felt awful.
Dragging herself out of bed, she located her thermometer in
her medicine chest and stuck it under her tongue. In the
mirror, her face looked flushed. Her throat was sore, and
every muscle in her body ached. Her thermometer read
ninety-seven point eight. So why was she feeling like she
wanted to lie down and die?

She had two cases this morning, and nothing special
scheduled this afternoon. Perhaps, after the O.R., she'd go

home and rest. If one of the junior residents was available, perhaps she'd skip operating today entirely.

She forced herself to get dressed and to drive to the hospital. Luck was with her. Her first case had been canceled, and she was able to assign the second to a third-year resident. She stopped into the department office and told the chairman's secretary that she was taking a sick day.

From there, she headed upstairs to Pathology to see if Larry had anything new to tell her.

Larry took one look at her and pulled out a chair.

"You look like someone just discharged you from the ICU. What's wrong?"

"Total body pain. I'm probably coming down with some virus."

"Have you considered seeing a doctor?"

"A doctor?"

"You know, one of those funny people in the white coats with a stethoscope. The internal medicine kind. I'm sure you're a great OB-GYN, but an infectious disease expert you're not."

"I thought I'd just go home and sleep it off."

"I have a better idea. Lots of the residents go to Marian Mitchell. She's competent, and nice, and her office is right across the street. Why don't I call and see if she can squeeze you in?"

Alanna felt too miserable to argue. Larry picked up the phone.

"She can see you at ten," Larry said. "In the meantime, I'm going to buy you some breakfast."

"That's sweet of you. Before I forget, I came up to see if you'd had a chance to run that PCR."

"I did. Your instincts were exactly right. Belinda Lancaster died because someone injected amniotic fluid into her. The fetal cells in her lungs are an exact match for one of the samples you gave me."

Alanna exhaled a low whistle. That was an awesome finding. "Which one?"

Larry consulted his notes and scribbled down the patient's name and hospital number. Alanna recognized it immediately. It was the patient whose amniocentesis had been performed by Lisa Keating.

"Killing someone this way takes a good deal of medical knowledge, plus access to the amnio lab. My bet is we're looking for a doctor, a nurse, or a pharmacist," Larry said.

"I agree. Do you think the same person was responsible for Suzanne Saunders?"

"It's certainly possible. Now that we know Lancaster was murdered, we should notify the police."

Alanna shook her head. "Maybe we can come up with a suspect first. Why don't we review both charts, make a list of all the nurses and physicians involved, and see if there's any overlap?"

"I don't think that's such a good idea. I only read detective novels. I'm not interested in participating in the real thing. Did it occur to you that chasing after a killer could be dangerous?"

"I'm not proposing we chase after anyone. All I want to do is review some charts, and frankly, I think I can do that more intelligently than some cop with a high school education. If you don't want to help me, I'll do it myself."

"Okay, you win. I'll help, but promise me you'll go to the police once we've got all the data together. We should also find out the pharmacy protocols for setting up those morphine pumps. I can do some of that. You need to get some rest."

"I'm not arguing," Alanna said. She hadn't mentioned to

Larry that Lisa Keating had done the amniocentesis. She couldn't believe that Lisa, much as she disliked her personally, could do such a thing. She wasn't going to point a finger without some hard evidence. She also couldn't tell Larry about the Penicillin that Arthur Underwood had accidentally received. Jeremy had told her that in confidence. She'd do her own research on that piece of the puzzle.

Larry took her to the coffee shop where she forced down some scrambled eggs, toast, and juice. The food made her feel better. At least her stomach wasn't upset.

"You know, there are two kinds of doctors," Larry said. "The ones who ignore all their symptoms and pretend it isn't happening because they think they're indispensable. I have a feeling you belong in that category."

He grinned at her. "Then, there are the ones like me who are born hypochondriacs. When I was a medical student, I had symptoms of practically every disease in Harrison's *Principles of Internal Medicine*."

"Even AIDS?"

"Are you kidding? I was convinced I had cardiomyopathy, Rocky Mountain spotted fever, and Hodgkin's Disease. You name it, I conjured it."

"You're trying to tell me something," Alanna said.

"You bet. I'm trying to tell you it's okay to take care of yourself when you're not feeling well. It's even okay to let someone else take care of you." He reached across the table and squeezed her hand.

"I'd better go. I'll be late for my appointment."

While she was sitting in Dr. Mitchell's waiting room, she took her notebook out of her jacket pocket and looked at the calendar. She noted the dates of Lancaster's and Saunders' deaths, and the date of Underwood's episode. Then she checked her OB-GYN call schedule. Lisa Keating had been on call all three nights. She wondered what possible motive Lisa could have had. It made no sense to her.

Dr. Mitchell gave her a thorough physical exam and told her she'd live provided she got some antibiotics for her strep throat.

"Residents are all alike. You drive yourselves into the ground, force yourselves to work no matter how sick you are, and then you wonder why you're walking around with every joint and muscle screaming in protest. Get a few days of rest," she ordered.

Alanna stopped at the pharmacy and returned to the hospital. On her way to the elevator, she ran into Gabrielle, looking glum, and bringing a lunch tray up from the coffee shop.

"Busy day in Labor and Delivery?"

Gaby made a face. "Even busier because my beloved junior resident didn't bother showing up for work this morning."

"Lisa?"

"Who else?"

"What was her excuse this time?" Alanna asked.

"She didn't bother to call and offer one. No one's been able to reach her. She's not home and she's not answering her beeper. How much do you want to bet Magnussen won't do a thing about it? She'll get away with this the same way she gets away with everything else. And, to add to a perfect day, a lovely woman I put a cerclage in just showed up with ruptured membranes in booming labor. She lost the baby. I told her MediCal doctor to send her home with a home uterine monitor, but did he listen?"

"Of course not. Some doctors would send a patient home the day after a heart transplant if the insurance company only allowed one day. I'm sorry about your patient, Gaby."

"Especially since it could have been prevented." Gaby marched down the hall and through the double doors to the delivery suite. Alanna entered the women's locker room.

The locker room, usually noisy and chaotic at seven in the morning, before surgery, was deserted at noon. Alanna opened her locker, hung up her white coat, and retrieved her purse. She paused, remembering that Lisa's locker was next to hers.

Glancing at it, she saw that its Yale lock appeared open. It was unlikely Lisa had left anything in it that would provide useful information, but it couldn't hurt to look. She opened Lisa's locker and quickly closed her own. If anyone saw her, they would assume the open locker was hers. Its contents were sparse: a pair of Nikes covered in blue paper shoe covers, a copy of William's Obstetrics, the classic reference text, and a white lab coat. There was a pile of surgical gloves on the locker floor.

Lisa's coat pockets contained two pens, her beeper, and a small, elegant maroon leather Filofax. Alanna unzipped it. Most residents carried similar notebooks, but few were as neatly organized as Lisa's. It looked brand new.

Alanna skimmed the calendar. It was this year's, and empty except for January. The initials SM were scattered in several places. She noted an appointment with someone named Geneva Jensen, which was underlined twice. Lisa's call schedule was penciled in. The telephone directory was almost blank. Lisa had not gotten around to transferring any numbers into it. All it contained was a few hospital extensions. There were two scraps of paper in the side pocket. One said "703". The other contained her locker number and computer passcode to access the hospital system. Alanna made a note of the numbers and replaced the scraps.

The only other thing in the Filofax was a checkbook. The check register went back an entire year and was filled out in a neat, girlish hand. Nothing that looked unusual; rent, phone, gas and electric, credit card bills, checks to Saks, Niemann, and several Rodeo Drive boutiques.

The magnitude of the checks, however, caught Alanna's eye. She scanned the deposits. The salary checks were deposited at the beginning of the month. The amounts were familiar. In addition, three thousand dollars a month appeared around the fifteenth. She wondered if Lisa's family supplemented her income. It was too round a number to be a moonlighting check.

She turned to January and was startled to see two ten-thousand-dollar deposits. The first was two days after Belinda Lancaster was murdered. The second, two days after Suzanne Saunders overdosed. Alanna copied down the dates, the bank account number, and the amounts. Then she replaced the Filofax and locked the door.

Her next stop was medical records. She requested her unsigned charts, and while waiting, she accessed the hospital database and looked up a hospital number for Arthur Underwood.

"Could you pull this one as well?" she asked the clerk.

He made a note of the number and grabbed the chart, adding it to Alanna's substantial pile. She took her charts to a secluded table and started signing. When she was done, she opened Underwood's chart and started a new page in her notebook.

After copying the names of all the doctors and nurses who had made notes in the chart, and the name of the pharmacist who had prepared Underwood's medication, she logged on to the hospital system once again.

Most residents used it only for lab results or room location. Alanna, however, had been curious enough and computer-savvy enough to learn a great deal more. As Chief Resident, her passcode allowed her access to most of the routine information. She was only prohibited from Quality Assurance data, legal information compiled by risk management, and confidential financial data.

Working her way into the nursing department files, she obtained the nurse schedule for the seventh floor on the night of the Underwood incident and cross-checked it with the nurse schedule for Obstetrics and Gynecology on the other two nights in question. The three lists had no overlap.

She repeated the exercise with the resident on-call schedule for the department of surgery and the pharmacy schedule. There had been three different pharmacists involved. None of the residents overlapped, except for Lisa Keating. Of course, all this could be meaningless. The murderer wasn't necessarily working those nights. It was easy to move around the hospital in a white coat. You blended in, and no one noticed you. It could be anybody.

She took one more careful look at Underwood's chart, and this time she was rewarded. Underwood had been hospitalized in room 703.

49

———

February 2, 1996, 9:15 a.m.
Los Angeles, California

MOSHER AND ROTH FACED EACH OTHER IN THE cubicle of Murray's office and compared notes.

"The hospitals check out clean," Roth said. "I can account for every single vial of Ketamine the manufacturer says they sold."

"I sent guys to check out all the places on the customer list. They were mostly vets and animal labs. No discrepancies between what they bought from the supply companies and what the supply companies can account for," Murray said. "You got the manufacturer's shipping list?"

Roth passed the printout across the table. Murray grabbed a pencil and checked the numbers for all the medical supply companies. The number of vials sold plus vials on hand should equal the number shipped by the manufacturer. He calculated and checked them off, one by one. "Bingo!"

"What?"

"The Health Web Medical Supply Company is missing a dozen vials of Ketamine. Look."

Roth leaned over and checked Murray's addition. "No shit. You sure?"

"Positive. I counted their entire stock myself. Twice."

Murray sorted through his files, pulled up the employee list he'd obtained from the company, and handed it to Roth. "Have someone run all these names. See if anyone has a record and find out if the company or any of its employees own a 1995 black Dodge Caravan."

When he left, Murray picked up the phone and called Santiago at the County Coroner's office.

"He's doing an autopsy," Santiago's secretary said, "but he's almost done. He wants you to come over."

"I was afraid you were going to say that," Murray said. "Tell him I'll be there in twenty."

50

———

February 2, 1996, 5:45 p.m.
Los Angeles, California

THE CLOCK SAID FIVE FORTY-FIVE WHEN Alanna awakened from her long afternoon nap and considered the pros and cons of dragging herself out of bed. She felt a little better, but just marginally. The thought of moving her body at all was highly unappealing.

The ring of her telephone forced her to roll over and reach for the receiver.

"Hi, it's Larry," a cheerful voice said. "Are you feeling any better?"

"I feel somewhere between moribund and dead, but thanks for asking."

"Have you had anything to eat or drink since I force-fed you breakfast?"

"I don't think so."

"What did Dr. Mitchell say?"

"She applied leeches, bled me, subjected me to lethal

148

radiation, then told me to take an Anaprox and call her in the morning."

"What did she really say?"

"That it was strep throat and I should take some antibiotics and a few days off."

"Do you have anyone at home to fuss over you? A roommate or something?"

"Not really. I live alone."

"In that case, I volunteer to come over with a bowl of chicken soup and a matzoh ball from Jerry's Deli. It cures everything. You sound like you could use a nurse."

Alanna didn't hesitate. "That's too thoughtful an offer to turn down."

She gave him her address and dragged herself to the bathroom, where she splashed cold water on her face and ran a comb through her hair. As an afterthought, she removed the sweat-soaked scrubs she'd fallen asleep in and changed into a clean pair of pajamas. She took her temperature again. Only a slight fever. Making her way to the kitchen, she opened her almost empty refrigerator and swallowed a large glass of ice water and another antibiotic.

By the time Larry rang the bell, she was feeling a little better. Maybe this was a twenty-four-hour thing.

"This is nice of you," she said. "I just realized my refrigerator's pretty empty, and I am starting to feel hungry."

Larry's kind face lit up. "I'm starving myself. Why don't you curl up on that sofa and let room service take care of you for a while?"

He settled her in the living room, tucked a blanket over her legs, and unpacked the brown grocery bag he'd brought. Making himself completely at home in her kitchen, he poured a bowl of chicken soup and a glass of orange juice and brought her dinner on a tray. He settled himself in the armchair opposite her with a corned beef sandwich.

"I thought you might be interested in a few things I discovered today. I had a long talk with one of the pharmacists who covers the surgical unit. I asked him about how the morphine pumps are made up.

"All the controlled drugs, including morphine, are kept in the secure drug room of each floor's satellite pharmacy. The door is locked at all times.

"There's a protocol for mixing the I.V. fluids for the analgesia pumps. Once the fluid is mixed up, the pharmacist places it in the delivery pump and programs the pump so that an overdose is impossible. The pumps are never left unlocked and unattended in the pharmacy.

"What about when the pump was in the patient's room? Could someone have added morphine to the I.V. fluid then?"

"Once the pump is opened, it won't deliver any medicine. Anyway, the police lab took the pump with them when they took Saunders' body to the County Coroner's office. I called the pathologist who did her autopsy. The morphine concentration in the bag was exactly what it was supposed to be, and the pump was still programmed.

"The police theory is that Saunders, who has a history of drug use, brought some of her stuff and gave herself an accidental overdose. When they searched, they found a syringe with morphine traces in it in the wastebasket next to her bedside."

"That's exactly where I'd put it if I'd just injected someone with a lethal dose and wanted it to look self-administered," Alanna said. "Did he say if they found any fingerprints on the syringe?"

"I didn't think to ask, but if you think it's important, I'll try to find out."

"I'm no detective, but wouldn't you expect to see her thumbprint on the plunger if she injected herself?"

"I have no idea. You've read more mystery novels than I have. I went through Belinda's chart. I've got a list of everyone directly involved with her care, but Saunders' chart isn't available. Risk management has it locked up. Anyway, there's no proof that the police theory is wrong. Maybe it was just a coincidence."

Alanna shook her head and placed the empty bowl of chicken soup on the coffee table beside her. "I don't believe it."

"Well, you're not going to prove it tonight. Dr. Larry recommends you get some sleep and worry about it tomorrow." He cleared the plates and stacked them in her dishwasher.

"I can't thank you enough," Alanna said. "I didn't think doctors still made house calls."

"Only for very special patients." Larry smiled at her, extricating himself from a chair. "I don't want to overstay my welcome. Feel better." He bestowed a light kiss on her forehead.

She locked her door behind him, shut the lights in the living room and kitchen, and retreated to her bedroom. The food, the information, and the afternoon nap had left her too wired to sleep.

Why hadn't she shared her suspicions about Lisa with Larry? Two heads were certainly better than one, and she wasn't all that fond of her fellow resident. The more she thought about it, the more certain she was that she was dealing with a physician.

All physicians knew about drug overdoses and anaphylactic reactions to drugs. Most nurses and pharmacists would as well. But amniotic fluid embolism was a rare complication, the sort of thing only an obstetrician might think of.

Lisa had the knowledge and the access to both the sample and the patient. It was interesting that she had been on call that night, yet Alanna couldn't remember seeing her at Belinda's Code Blue. Why hadn't she come running the way all the other residents had?

Could she have been responsible for the other two incidents? Alanna tried putting herself in Lisa's place. How would she get hold of morphine? Easily. It was always available on the anesthesiologists' carts, and anesthesiologists varied in how compulsive they were about locking them.

If you were in an operating room, it would be easy to lift a vial while the anesthesiologist was in pre-op with the patient, or even while he was occupied intubating. As a physician, no one would question your presence or your activities. No one would even notice.

What about the antibiotics? Patient allergies were always prominently displayed on the chart, and antibiotics weren't kept under lock and key. Alanna had passed the pharmacy any number of times when the door was open and the pharmacist was elsewhere. How hard could it be to steal a bottle of penicillin and an I.V. bag to dissolve it in? The tricky part would be substituting it for the drug Underwood was supposed to have. She wasn't quite sure how she would have accomplished that.

That left the most important question still unanswered. What possible motive could Lisa Keating have had?

She yawned. Maybe she could figure that part out tomorrow.

51

———

February 5, 1996, 11:00 a.m.
Los Angeles, California

THE GIRL IN THE MORGUE WAS IDENTIFIED TWO days later. A recent entry into the Missing Persons File of the National Crime Information Center database matched the information Mosher placed into the Unidentified Persons File.

"Her name is Lisa Keating," Murray told his team. "Doctor Lisa Keating. She's a resident in obstetrics and gynecology at Los Angeles Memorial Hospital. The head of her program reported that she was missing when she failed to turn up for work two days in a row."

"She has an apartment in Beverly Hills on South Doheny, drives a 1995 Jaguar Sedan, and has three outstanding parking violations. No other record. Her parents' home is in Dallas. I've asked the police department there to notify her next of kin. We'll need someone at the hospital to come down and make a formal identification of the body. "

"I tried calling the medical staff office and the office of the hospital president, but all I got was a damn phone machine. Roth, you'll have to drive down there and get hold of the director of her residency program. I want him here tonight. The rest of you, come with me. We've got a warrant to search the doctor's apartment. Call me when you're back at the station with Dr. Keating's boss. I want to question him."

Lisa Keating lived in a spacious, modern one-bedroom apartment, expensively and eclectically furnished. Murray estimated the square footage at twice that of his bungalow.

The kitchen was a narrow galley, spotlessly clean. Murray opened drawers and cabinets, removing the drawers from their slots, checking underneath them for hidden papers, and opening and exploring every container. The kitchen contained a respectable collection of wine, scotch, and whiskey, a few cans of soup, and some breakfast cereal. The refrigerator was stocked with frozen dinners and diet drinks.

The doctor may have had excellent taste in furniture, but it seemed doubtful she ever bothered to prepare a meal. Leaving the crime scene techs to look inside sofa cushions and dust for fingerprints, Murray sought out the bedroom.

It was as expensively furnished as the rest of the apartment. Murray went to the closet. It was packed with designer clothes, neatly hung by type and color. Shoes and accessories were organized in see-through plastic boxes and labeled with typewritten labels. It would take a while to check inside the pockets of all those expensive suits and purses.

The bathroom gave the only clue that someone lived there. A thick terry bath sheet was draped over the shower stall. A hair dryer, still plugged in, lay on the sink. The medicine chest contained assorted medications in small bottles, all of which said "sample, not for sale." The drawer below the sink contained a diaphragm, jelly, and toothpaste.

Murray returned to the bedroom and turned his attention to the desk and phone. The drawers yielded nothing of interest other than a Rolodex, which Murray put in an evidence bag for future perusal. The pile of papers contained mostly bills and catalogs, no letters. There were several messages on the answering machine. Murray replayed them.

"Lisa, this is Gabrielle Broder. It's after eight-thirty, and it would be nice if you reported to labor and delivery. I've tried paging and beeping you. If you're home, please answer this."

Gabrielle Broder, whoever she was, sounded pissed off. He made a note of her name, intending to talk to her himself.

"Dr. Keating, this is Geneva Jensen calling. I have a few points I need to clarify. Please call my office at your convenience."

Murray made a note of that name as well. It sounded familiar, but he couldn't place it.

The third and last caller was male and sounded older and authoritative. "Lisa, this is Dr. Magnussen. I understand you are not in the hospital today. Be good enough to call me when you get this message."

As a final measure, Murray pushed the redial button on Lisa's phone. It connected to a honeyed, Southern female voice.

"Health Web Incorporated, how can I help you?"

By the time Mosher returned to Parker Center, Roth had arrived with Sherman Magnussen and had seated the doctor in one of the tiny interview areas adjacent to the squad room.

"He was able to identify her," Roth said. "Poor guy turned white as a sheet when he saw the body. I was afraid he'd throw up all over the morgue."

"I'll try to put him out of his misery quickly," Murray said.

"Find anything at the girl's apartment?"

"Maybe. You'll never guess what I got when I pushed the redial button on her phone. The corporate offices of Health Web in Dallas."

"That's where she's from, isn't it?"

Murray nodded. "Funny how that company keeps cropping up. Why don't you show your guest into my office? I'd like you to tape what he tells us."

Magnussen, his lips tightly compressed and his face pale, shook hands with Mosher and seated himself across the desk, pulling up the gray gabardine knees of his trousers as he crossed his legs.

"I'll try not to keep you too long, doctor. I know this has been an ordeal for you. I'd like to ask you a few questions. I hope you can help with our investigation. My associate will tape what you tell us. It will help us to remember information."

"Tape what you want," Magnussen said. "I can't believe anything like this could happen to Dr. Keating."

"We'll do our best to find out, sir. What can you tell us about Dr. Keating? Did you know her well?"

"I knew her as well as any of my other residents. This

was her third year. She was a hard worker, well-liked, and a good clinician. Patients were drawn to her. She had an excellent manner."

"Who were her friends?"

He shook his head. "I can tell you the names of all the other residents, but I don't pay attention to their relationships with one another. I know nothing about Lisa's personal life."

"Did she have a boyfriend?"

"I have no idea. She was attractive. She may have had, but I never saw her with anyone. I'm sorry. I'm not being very helpful. You understand the chairman is the last person to hear departmental gossip. I'm sure you'll do better when you speak to the residents."

"When was the last time you saw her?"

Magnussen's voice took on a helpful tone. "I believe it was Monday. I recall she came to my office."

"And do you remember the conversation?"

"She was upset about Suzanne Saunders. You may have read about her unfortunate death in the papers. Lisa assisted with her surgery and knew the patient well."

"And how did the patient die?"

"I don't know yet. The autopsy result isn't in. That's what I told Lisa at the time. I promised to let her know as soon as I had an answer."

"Did she tell you anything about her plans for Friday evening?"

"No. As I said, I was her chairman. It wasn't the sort of thing she would mention to me."

"You called her yesterday morning. Why was that?"

Magnussen uncrossed and recrossed his legs. "She hadn't shown up for work. The other residents notified me, and naturally, I was concerned. It isn't like a resident to skip work without telling us. I thought perhaps she was ill."

"You didn't consider reporting her missing, or having someone check her apartment?"

"I guess I wasn't that worried, detective. I couldn't reach her. I got involved in other activities, and before I knew it, it was evening. I figured she'd be in the next morning. When she wasn't, some of her fellow residents requested that I notify the police. Can I leave now? I'm exhausted and upset, and I don't think I have anything useful to tell you."

"Of course, doctor. We may need to talk to you again. We do need all the information on your resident staff."

"Do you need it tonight, or can I have my secretary give you a complete list in the morning?"

"I think morning will do," Murray said. "No point in rousting them out of bed now. Thank you."

"You didn't ask him if he knew she was recently pregnant," Roth said after Magnussen left.

Murray shook his head. "That's a detail we'll hold for now. At the moment, very few people are aware of that fact, and one of them is the killer."

52

─────────

February 6, 1996, 6:00 a.m.
Los Angeles, California

ALANNA WOKE AT HER USUAL TIME, FEELING considerably better. Amazing, how a day or two in bed and some chicken soup could brighten your whole perspective.

While her coffee was brewing, she put on a pair of slacks and a bright blue, cotton-knit sweater. Opening her front door, she retrieved her morning paper and set it on the kitchen table with her favorite mug. She sliced a bagel, popped it in the toaster, and slathered it with cream cheese.

What a sweetheart Larry had been, to bring her dinner the other night, and to leave these for breakfast. Pouring her coffee, she settled herself at the table and skimmed the headlines. Nothing caught her interest until she picked up the Metro section.

MEMORIAL PHYSICIAN FOUND MURDERED
The nude, dead body of obstetrical resident, Dr. Lisa

Keating was found Wednesday night under the Brooklyn Avenue off-ramp of the San Bernardino Freeway...

The details of the article were sketchy. The police had revealed nothing about the cause of death. The paper mentioned Lisa's hometown, Dallas, and included a quote from Dr. Magnussen stating that Lisa had been an outstanding physician, and he was shocked and saddened at her death.

No wonder Lisa hadn't shown up for work. Had her death been a random piece of Los Angeles violence, or could it, in some mysterious way, be connected to the other deaths at Memorial? Alanna felt nauseated. Much as she had personally disliked Lisa, no one deserved to die like this.

This answered the question of whether Alanna was going to work today. With Lisa gone, the department would be short a resident, and the others would need all the help they could get.

53

February 6, 1996, 8:00 a.m.
Los Angeles, California

MOSHER AND ROTH, ACCOMPANIED BY TWO police officers, arrived at Los Angeles Memorial Hospital at eight o'clock sharp and presented themselves at the chairman's office. They obtained a list of Lisa Keating's fellow residents and divided it in half, agreeing that they would concentrate on finding out who her friends and possibly a lover were. Murray commandeered a conference room down the hall from Labor and Delivery for his staff and decided to begin with Gabrielle Broder.

Mosher was intrigued by the stunning blonde who seated herself opposite him with great composure.

"We were shocked to hear about Lisa Keating, Detective. How can I help you?"

"Were you and Dr. Keating friends?"

"I was her chief resident on obstetrics, but I wouldn't say we were friends."

"Friendly?"

Gabrielle hesitated. "No. We weren't friendly."

"Could you tell me who her good friends were among the residents? Was she well-liked?"

There was a long pause. Something, Murray decided, was not quite right. The pause was long enough for Mosher to note that Dr. Broder was measuring her words.

"Doctor, you'll help me a great deal more by being frank than by being tactful. Please."

"Well, honestly, I don't think Lisa Keating had any friends among the residents. No one liked her very much."

"Including you?"

"Including me, I'm afraid. It feels uncomfortable saying things like this about someone who has just died."

Murray tried to reassure her. "Nothing you say will go outside of this room, Dr. Broder. Please tell me why you, in particular, disliked her."

"She was a bad doctor. She was lazy, irresponsible, and made dangerous mistakes. I always had to look over her shoulder when I was in charge to be certain she didn't do something that could seriously hurt a patient. She spent a great deal of time ingratiating herself with wealthy patients and with people around the hospital who were in positions of power to advance her career. She never did her share of the work. Residents don't like it much when they get dumped on by their colleagues."

This was more than Mosher expected. "If she were such a poor physician, why did they keep her in the residency program?"

Gabrielle Broder raised her eyebrows. "Are you kidding. She had the chairman wrapped around her little finger. He thought she walked on water. He let her get away with anything she wanted, regardless of how unfair it was to the other residents."

"It sounds as if she made a few enemies," Mosher said. "Did all the residents hate her?"

"Hate is too strong a term," she said thoughtfully. "I would describe it more as contempt. No one respected or trusted her. I certainly can't imagine that anyone felt strongly enough about her to kill her, if that's what you're implying."

"I wasn't implying anything. Do you know if she dated or had a special boyfriend?"

"She didn't confide in me. Maybe one of the other residents knows. Actually..." she hesitated.

Murray waited. Silence, he had found, was an effective interviewing tool.

"I'm not sure this is relevant, but several years ago, in medical school, she had an affair with Nick, my ex-husband."

"After you were divorced?"

"Before we were married. I don't know if it continued while we were married or not. Nick screwed around with so many women, I lost track. That's why I divorced him. I don't have any reason to think they were involved recently, but Nick is in the Anesthesia department here. Maybe he knows something about her personal life."

"I'll check it out. You left a message on Lisa Keating's phone machine yesterday morning. Were you thinking that something might have happened to her? Were you worried?"

"To tell the truth, Detective, I wasn't worried. I was angry. I figured she'd decided to take the day off to go shopping or to a movie and hadn't bothered to inform anyone she wasn't coming in. It was completely in character. I never imagined in a million years that she was dead."

Mosher couldn't think of anything else to ask. He told her she could leave and asked her not to repeat their conversation.

54

February 6, 1996, 11:30 a.m.
Los Angeles, California

BY THE END OF THE MORNING, MOSHER AND Roth had interviewed all but one of the residents on their list. They decided to take a short break for lunch and to check messages. Murray brought up a tray of fried chicken and coleslaw from the cafeteria. Roth had egg salad on whole wheat with alfalfa sprouts and a container of non-fat milk.

Roth moved their tape recorder and a pile of papers to the side of the conference room table and took a bite of his sandwich.

"Interesting set of interviews. Last night, Magnussen said she was Florence Nightingale. Today, the residents wouldn't let her treat their pet rat. She seems to have been universally disliked."

Mosher nodded. "The question that interests me is whether the chairman believed what he told us or whether he was lying."

"I'm especially interested in the non-existent boyfriend," Roth said.

"Well, she was screwing around in med school with one of the anesthesiologists. We should talk to him as soon as he gets out of surgery. We've also got one more resident to talk to. If we draw a blank, we'll ask her parents. They're supposed to be flying in this afternoon."

"Someone was doing her."

Wiping his greasy hands on a large paper napkin, Murray agreed.

55

February 6, 1996, 1:30 p.m.
Los Angeles, California

AT ONE-THIRTY IN THE AFTERNOON, ALANNA appeared at the door of the conference room. It was opened for her by a wiry young policeman with sandy hair who seemed to be standing guard. Another man, older and apparently in charge, was seated inside at a table with a pile of papers and a tape recorder in front of him. He looked up through reading glasses, perched low on his nose, as Alanna entered the room.

"You must be Dr. Davidson. Thank you for coming. Have a seat, please."

Alanna chose the seat facing him and waited. A younger man with a round, boyish face and pale blonde hair was sitting unobtrusively in the corner with a notepad in front of him.

I'm Detective Mosher. This is my partner, Lieutenant Roger Roth. We're investigating the death of your colleague, Dr. Keating. I'm going to tape our conversation. It will make it easier for me to recall any specific information you might be able to help us with."

Alanna shrugged. "I don't know that I'll be of much help. I saw the news of Lisa's death in the paper this morning. No one in the hospital has been able to talk about anything else. How did she die, Detective Mosher? Was she shot?"

"I can't tell you that yet. I'm waiting for the autopsy. Do you happen to know anything about Dr. Keating's plans the evening of her death?"

"Nothing. I was home sick the day she died and the day after. I didn't see her at all."

"When was the last time you saw her?"

Alanna thought for a moment. "I believe it was last Friday. I saw her in the operating suite. She was scrubbing to help Dr. Magnussen on a case."

"Was that Suzanne Saunders?"

"Yes, it was."

"Do you recall your conversation with her?"

"Vaguely. I was surprised to see her operating because she was assigned to Labor and Delivery. I was running the gynecology service. I asked her what she was doing there, and she said that Dr. Magnussen had requested her assistance. I said okay, and I left the suite. That was the last time I saw her."

Mosher looked down at one of his papers and made a note. Alanna hesitated. Should she tell him, or would he think she was a fool playing amateur detective? What hard evidence did she actually have?

Lisa had been on call the night two patients had died. One was unquestionably murdered. She'd had access to the amniotic fluid that had killed Belinda Lancaster, and two days after each death, a large deposit had been made in her checking account

She couldn't tell him that part without admitting she had looked through Lisa's locker. There could be any number of other explanations for why she had that information, but Alanna decided to wait. Mosher's voice snapped her out of her thoughts.

"Were you friends with Lisa Keating?"

"No, I wasn't."

"Do you know who her friends were? Her boyfriend, perhaps?"

"I didn't know she had a boyfriend. I never gave it much thought."

"No one seems to know much about her personal life."

"Perhaps she kept her personal life private. Some people don't like to be gossiped about at work."

"Did you like Dr. Keating? Was she a good physician?"

Alanna hesitated, considered tact, and decided to tell the truth. "No, and no. I didn't like her personally, and I don't know anyone who did."

"And her medical skills?"

"Bordering on the dangerously incompetent. I always hated having her as my junior resident. It meant I had to do twice as much work. But I'm sure this isn't news to you, Detective. You've spoken to all the other residents already. I can't imagine anyone said anything nice."

She waited for Mosher's response, but he kept his face impassive. The flow of information was only going to be one way. Somehow, she didn't feel he'd be receptive to any of her theories. Keeping her mouth shut seemed to be the better part of valor.

"All right, Doctor. If you think of anything that might be helpful, please call me." He handed her his card. "Thank you."

Alanna rose and fled the room with relief.

Mosher smiled as Alanna left the room. Something about her reminded him of his daughter Michelle. They had the same kind of dark, good looks and the same straightforward manner. He'd missed Michelle since she'd moved to Boston for college.

Alanna's testimony had certainly been consistent with everyone else's. Only one more to go. While he waited for Nicholas Broder, Murray gathered his notes and tapes. He'd summarize everything and enter it into the murder book at the office.

Broder arrived a few moments later, a wiry man with thinning hair, wearing rumpled scrubs. He looked as if he could use a shave. He slid into the chair, crossing one leg over the opposite knee, revealing a navy-blue sock.

"What's this about, Detective?"

"I'm sure you know what it's about. Lisa Keating. We're interviewing everyone who knew her. We'll be recording your statement."

Broder ran a hand through his balding hair and turned his attention back to Mosher with a look that said he didn't much care what Mosher did.

The two of them stared at one another, Murray waiting to see if Broder would offer anything. When it became clear that nothing was forthcoming, he began.

"When did you last see Dr. Keating?"

"Last Friday was the last time I can remember. I was giving anesthesia to a patient of Dr. Magnussen's, and Lisa was the assistant surgeon."

"Would that have been Suzanne Saunders?"

"Yeah, that's right."

"I would imagine that, as an anesthesiologist, you get to

watch many surgeons operate. Was Lisa Keating a good surgeon?"

Broder raised his eyebrows. "That depends on how you define good. Lisa was original. She had ways of doing things that were unique to her. Some people criticized her for deviating from the standard technique. They thought she was a show-off and endangering patients by performing procedures whose worth and results hadn't been established by academic studies in the literature. Other people, like Magnussen, for example, admired her creativity."

"And what did you think?"

"I think my opinion of Lisa's surgical techniques is irrelevant to your investigation. Is there anything else you wanted to know?"

"Did she do any original surgery on Suzanne Saunders?"

"Are you kidding? Saunders was Magnussen's V.I.P. patient. Lisa only demonstrated her creativity on clinic patients."

"Any particular clinic patients?"

"I couldn't tell you. You might try medical records. You think she was done in by the Russian Mafia because her experimental bladder suspension on someone's grandmother fell down?"

Mosher was beginning to get annoyed. Lisa's clinic patients and their families could open up a whole new avenue of investigation, but he didn't appreciate Broder's wise ass attitude.

"What I think is my business, Doctor. I'm much more interested in what you think. Were you dating Lisa Keating?"

"No, I wasn't." Broder's posture didn't change, but Murray could see one of his facial muscles twitch at the question.

"Are you sure, Doctor? It seems to be a matter of common knowledge around the hospital that the two of you were an item a few years ago."

"That was a few years ago, Detective. I've been married, divorced, and dated lots of women since then."

"What was she like, socially? Why did you stop seeing her?"

"Not my type. She was cold, ambitious, selfish, and, if you must know, not very interesting in bed. Our relationship didn't last very long."

"Do you know if she was seeing anyone recently? Anyone from the hospital?"

Broder shrugged and glanced at his watch. "I don't have a clue. She didn't confide in me. Are we done yet? I need to be in the O.R. in five minutes."

Mosher was tempted to make him late just for the fun of it, but that probably wouldn't be fair to the patient. The bastard was hiding something, and Mosher could deal with his arrogance.

As soon as Broder left the room, Mosher made himself a note to call the doctor downtown for more questioning. He would also question Lisa Keating's parents about Broder.

56

———

February 6, 1996, 6:00 p.m.
Los Angeles, California

Back at Parker Center, Mosher checked his messages, washed his face, combed his unruly hair, and prepared himself to meet with the bereaved parents. The secretary escorted them into his small office.

"This is Dorothy and Henry Peterson, sir, Dr. Keating's mother and stepfather."

Mosher rose, shook hands with Mr. Peterson, and motioned for them to sit. Hank Peterson was a tall, fair man with graying blonde hair receding from a high, sunburned forehead. He wore a light gray suit with a pale blue shirt that matched his eyes. The eyes darted around the office, and his large, hairy hands tapped incessantly on his knees.

"Do you mind if I light a cigarette?" he asked.

Mosher passed an ashtray toward him. Peterson's hands shook as he removed a cigarette from a handsome silver case in his breast pocket and lit it with a matching lighter. Inhaling the smoke seemed to calm him.

Dorothy Peterson was tall and slim, about fifty, Mosher judged, with a body that was still voluptuous. Her black hair was drawn back into a severe French twist, and she wore a navy suit with no jewelry. Her face would have been quite striking, except for her puffy and bloodshot eyes. Mosher could see where Lisa Keating had gotten her good looks. She sat poker-straight in the uncomfortable wooden chair, her hands clasped tightly in her lap.

"I can't tell you how sorry I am for your loss," Mosher said.

"When can we take our little girl home?" Henry said.

"Whenever you wish. The autopsy is complete. You can arrange to fly her body to Dallas immediately."

"Have you caught the monster who did this?" Dorothy said.

"Not yet, Mrs. Peterson, but we have some leads. I want to share some information with you that we are keeping confidential. Perhaps you can help us. Your daughter was pregnant when she died, and it appears that the killer may have been responsible for aborting the pregnancy and then letting her bleed to death.

"No one has been able to identify any man who could have been the father of her child. I was hoping you might know who she dated."

Mosher fixed his gaze on Lisa's mother. She stared at the floor, her lips tightly pressed together, tears sliding down her cheeks. Finally, she regained a measure of composure and looked up.

"Lisa was a beautiful, popular girl. She had a million boyfriends in high school and at the University of Texas. Different ones would come and go practically every week. In college, she dated boys from all the best fraternities, but wasn't serious about any of them."

"What about more recently, since she moved to California?"

"I'd ask her all the time if there was someone special, but she'd just laugh at me. I kept telling her those little eggs in her ovaries weren't getting any younger, and she'd better find a nice, rich doctor and settle down. She didn't seem to have anyone special, or be in a hurry to find someone."

"Did she ever mention a man named Nicholas Broder?"

"Not that I recall."

"What about you, Mr. Peterson? Did your daughter ever confide in you about her social life?"

Peterson shook his head. "Lisa and I weren't as close as I would have liked. Her real daddy died when she was five, and I married Dorothy here when Lisa was sixteen. I think she resented me. I understood, of course. No one could replace her real daddy, but she was always cool and distant to me. I saw her just a few weeks ago, took her to dinner, but she didn't tell me anything that would help you."

"Where did you see her?"

"I was in Los Angeles doing business. I always try to call her when I'm here. We went to one of those California cuisine places--you know, goat cheese on everything."

"What kind of business are you in, Mr. Peterson?"

Peterson removed a slim wallet from his jacket and took out a card. He slid it across the desk to Mosher. "I'm in health care acquisitions. Vice President of Health Web Incorporated. You may have heard of us. We have several clinics in your area, and we're looking to buy a hospital."

"Yes, I have heard of you. What hospital are you planning to buy?"

Peterson hesitated. "You understand, this is confidential information, but we're currently negotiating with Los

Angeles Memorial. It is the finest hospital in the city, and we'd like to add it to the Health Web family."

"Interesting. What did your daughter think of the possibility?"

"Oh, I never discussed business with Lisa."

"Did your daughter call you at work this week?"

Peterson shook his head. "Lisa never called me at work. When she called, she always called home to talk to her mother."

"Did she call you, ma'am?" Mosher asked, turning to Dorothy.

"No," Dorothy whispered. "I hadn't talked to her in weeks."

"Did she have any special girlfriends? Anyone at all she might have confided in?"

"Well," Dorothy said, "the only person I can think of is Karen Kaye Miller. Her family lives next door to us. She was Lisa's best friend when they were children, and they were roommates in college. I called her yesterday after we heard, and she was devastated. Karen Kaye lives in Fort Worth now. She married a nice boy right after college, and they have three children. I could give you her number."

"I'd appreciate that very much, ma'am. I won't keep you any longer. If you think of anything else, please call me. I promise I'll keep you fully informed of the investigation."

Henry Peterson rose and shook hands again. His palm was damp. Dorothy took a tissue from her purse and dabbed her eyes.

Mosher called for one of the department clerks to guide them through the red tape of obtaining Lisa's body and shut his office door behind him. God, of all the things he had to do as a homicide detective, consoling the bereaved was the part that made him feel least competent.

More and more pieces were appearing on the table, but Mosher had no idea how to put them together. Health Web was attempting to buy Los Angeles Memorial. Lisa Keating had been a resident there. Her father was Vice President, and her last call before she died had been to Health Web, although not to her father.

Health Web also owned a medical supply company that happened to be a bit short on Ketamine, the drug that The Surgeon had been using on his victims. Lisa was another of those victims. But how did she tie into the homeless man, the drunk, and the hooker who had preceded her? It couldn't all be a coincidence. There had to be a pattern.

He reached for the phone and called the Dallas police department. He'd try to get hold of the cops who had broken the news to the Petersons. He needed someone to interview the receptionist at Health Web. If Lisa hadn't been phoning her father, Mosher wanted to know who she'd spoken to.

57

February 7, 1996, 6:00 p.m.
Los Angeles, California

A LANNA WALKED DOWN TO THE NURSING station, pulled the charts of the two patients she'd operated on that morning, and checked their vital signs. On paper, at least, everything appeared stable. Taking her stethoscope out of her pocket, she draped it around her neck and knocked softly at the door of one of her two post-ops.

After determining that both were doing well, she returned to the nursing station, wrote her notes and orders, and contemplated her next move. The thing that was bothering her the most was Lisa Keating's death. Could her suspicion about Lisa's involvement in the other hospital deaths have been wrong? Could Lisa have been on the trail of the hospital killer and been killed when she got too close?

Or could Lisa have been responsible for the killings with an accomplice who eliminated her for his protection? She couldn't think of what to do next. It seemed that at least in the hospital, she had come to a dead end.

The other thing disturbing her was that odd-looking machine she'd discovered at Health Web. It had haunted her dreams ever since she'd glimpsed it. She wondered if Justin Washington knew anything about it.

Checking her watch, she realized it was almost six o'clock, time for turnover rounds on Labor and Delivery. That meant Justin would be leaving any minute. If she went over there now, she might catch him.

As she hurried down the hall, she noticed Gabrielle walking in the same direction. She quickened her pace and caught up with her.

"I haven't seen you since Lisa was killed. Are you managing to run obstetrics with just two junior residents?"

Gaby shrugged. "With all the help I got from Lisa, I've been running obstetrics with a staff of two for months. Did the police interview you?"

"They did. I didn't have much to tell them. You?"

Gaby nodded. "Listen, if you promise not to tell, I'll confess. I did something nasty."

"You? You don't know the meaning of the word nasty."

"I'm trying to learn," Gaby said. "I told the police that Nick and Lisa had an affair a few years ago."

"They did? How come you never told me?" That was a very interesting piece of information. It put a new slant on things.

"Nick had affairs with everyone. Lisa was just one of a crowd."

"Do you think he was seeing her recently?"

"I have no idea. That's for him to know and the police to find out." Gaby giggled. "I wish I could have been there during his interview."

Alanna smiled back as Gabrielle hit the control that opened the double doors to the delivery suite. She'd wait for

Justin outside. As she thought about it, she realized that Nick, as well as Lisa, had been involved in all three mysterious incidents.

He'd done the anesthesia for Belinda Lancaster, Suzanne Saunders, and Arthur Underwood, and he'd been the attending anesthesiologist the night Belinda had her cardiac arrest. He'd been in the perfect position to enter their rooms without suspicion, and he certainly was knowledgeable enough to engineer the deaths. Had Lisa somehow seen him, suspected, and been killed because of it? Alanna's head was beginning to spin.

Justin emerged from Labor and Delivery, his white coat slung over his shoulder, his briefcase heavy in his other hand.

"Got a minute?"

He looked exhausted, but he smiled at her. "What's up?"

"I started at Health Web this week," Alanna said. "Thanks for setting it up so quickly. The money's pretty good. I have a question for you. Have you ever had a feeling that something odd is going on at that clinic?"

"What kind of odd?" He bent and put down his briefcase, looking at her more carefully.

"It's just that those medical assistants don't seem very competent to me."

"You mean they strike you as kids who should be behind the counter at McDonald's instead of making medical decisions."

"You hit the nail on the head."

Justin picked up his briefcase again and started walking toward the elevator.

"This is the new medicine. Competent isn't the keyword. The keyword is cheap." Justin pressed the down button.

"Have you seen that funny-looking machine in the room

next door to the doctor's consult? I walked in there by mistake, and I thought Hauptmann would bite my head off."

Justin laughed. "The same thing happened to me." He held the elevator door open for Alanna to enter. "She says it's a special photography thing. They seem to take a lot of patients in there. I figured if they wanted me to know about it, they'd tell me. No point in ruining a good moonlighting job by being nosy."

"I suppose you're right. Are they open on Saturdays?"

"Nine to nine. Saturday and Sunday. Why? Do you want to work more hours?"

Alanna shook her head. "Just wondered." An idea was beginning to take shape, and she felt Justin wouldn't want to know about it.

58

February 7, 1996, 7:00 p.m.
Los Angeles, California

THE OPERATING ROOMS AT LOS ANGELES Memorial were closed for the day. Only a skeleton crew remained on call, prepared to deal with trauma from the emergency room or middle-of-the-night requests from surgeons whose patients insisted on having ruptured appendices or tubal pregnancies at inconvenient hours.

Nick Broder remained behind, meticulously organizing the contents of his anesthesia cart. His interview with the police had left him agitated and annoyed. They couldn't possibly suspect that he was responsible for Lisa's murder. Mosher's line about their affair being a matter of common knowledge had been bullshit. He'd dated Lisa long before either of them had come to Memorial.

He hoped the police had found his version of the relationship with Lisa convincing. He hadn't told them the real reason he'd dumped her. The truth was that Lisa had been dynamite in bed. He just didn't like her habit of using him as her source for exotic drugs. Nick liked to use, but he didn't like to share.

He crushed several used syringe wrappings in his fist and tossed them into the wastepaper basket. The syringes were sorted by size, and the needles by gauge. Preprinted labels for all the most common anesthesia meds lay beside them in colorful rolls.

The next drawer down contained his endotracheal tubes, intravenous, and arterial line equipment. He checked off his stock list. The top drawer contained his drug supply. Nick liked to be certain he had everything and enough of it when he started a case. You'd never catch him running out of something in the middle.

He seemed to be a bit short on morphine. He could have sworn he had six vials left. Had he taken one home? He couldn't remember. In any case, he'd better replace it before morning. You never knew when the police might decide to look through his drug drawer.

Nick took his key to the locked drug cabinet at the pharmacy and helped himself to two more vials. He placed one in the drawer and shut it. The other, he slipped into his back pocket. Then, he clamped the padlock that secured his cart and headed for the parking garage and home.

59

February 8, 1996, 10:00 a.m.
Los Angeles, California

GENEVA JENSON'S OFFICE WAS EXACTLY WHAT Mosher imagined a successful Beverly Hills law office would look like. An attractive receptionist sat behind an etched glass partition. She took Mosher and escorted him to Ms. Jenson's private conference room.

"Thank you for coming, Mr. Mosher." Geneva Jenson rose from behind her desk and shook his hand. "Please make yourself comfortable. Can I have my secretary get you some coffee?"

Mosher noticed a tray with two English China cups on a sideboard. There was a coffee machine, and the beverage smelled freshly made.

"I'd love some," he said. "The stuff down at the station house rots metal."

The receptionist placed the tray on Geneva's desk between them and poured. Mosher inhaled the fragrance and sipped with pleasure. Opposite him, Geneva Jenson was doing the same, leaning back in a black leather chair. She had an attractive face, unlined and without makeup. Her smile was warm, and Mosher found himself liking her despite his prejudices against Beverly Hills lawyers. He reached into his pocket for a notebook and a pen.

"You said that you had information about Lisa Keating."

"Detective, I don't know whether this information will be relevant to you or not. If it turns out that it has no bearing on this case, I want your word that it will not go beyond this room. I would not like to cause Dr. Keating's family any further pain or embarrassment."

"I understand. I think I can safely promise you that anything you tell me that I don't already know will stay between us unless I need it to find or convict the killer."

Geneva leaned an elbow on her desk and ran her fingers through her hair. She looked agitated. Mosher imagined that her clients did not often turn up murdered.

"Dr. Keating came to see me on Wednesday evening. She had decided to file a sexual harassment suit against the chairman of her department, Sherman Magnussen. She stated that he had raped her several weeks previously, and as a result, she became pregnant. I presume you would have been aware of her pregnancy from the autopsy."

Mosher let out a satisfied grunt. "You've just solved one major mystery for me, Ms. Jenson. No one seemed to know who she was dating, or if she had a boyfriend. This would certainly explain it. Did she tell you what she planned to do about her pregnancy?"

"She wanted to abort as soon as possible. I told her to have the doctor save the tissue for genetic studies so that we could establish paternity."

"Did she tell you where she was planning to have her abortion?"

Geneva shook her head. "No, she didn't. Had she gone through with it before her death?"

"In a manner of speaking. Do you think Magnussen knew she was pregnant and planning to sue?"

"She told him she was pregnant. He was very cruel to her when he found out, and his reaction made her so angry that she decided to consult me. I have no idea if he knew that she was filing a lawsuit, but if he did, it occurred to me that he might have had a motive for murder. That's why I called you."

Even if he didn't know, the pregnancy alone could have been a motive. Married man, chairman of the department, pregnant resident. It would have been quite a scandal. It would have ruined his reputation. Her death couldn't have been timelier for him.

"Did she tell you anything else you think could be relevant?"

Geneva got up from her chair, went to the side table, and poured herself a second cup of black coffee. She stood there, brow furrowed, trying to remember.

"I don't think so," she said finally. "Our discussion was brief. I told her to try to find any other residents or employees harassed by Magnussen. Men like him rarely confine themselves to one victim. She said she'd try."

Mosher rose. It was getting late, and he was hungry and excited. "I can't thank you enough for calling me, Ms. Jenson. You've been a tremendous help."

Mosher's head was spinning. Not only did Magnussen have a perfect motive for Lisa Keating's murder, but he also had the medical knowledge to be The Surgeon. Had Geneva Jenson unknowingly identified the serial killer for him?

Tomorrow, Mosher would begin the background investigation that would hopefully link Magnussen to the other murders. He could question him again about Lisa's pregnancy, but he couldn't arrest him for her death without a lot more evidence.

60

———

February 9, 1996, 6:30 p.m.
Los Angeles, California

THE RAIN WAS COMING DOWN IN BLINDING sheets, obscuring the view from Alanna's patio and reducing it to a blur of streetlights on a dark background. She cracked open the patio door and was rewarded by a cold blast of wind. Shutting and locking it, she pulled the curtains and returned to the warm living room.

Southern California was the land of perpetual sunshine, punctuated with periodic winter storms that often flooded the Sepulveda basin, overran the storm drains, and sent mud and debris flying down the hillsides. Drivers, unused to bad weather, skidded dangerously even on the local streets, creating chaos. It was a good night to be home.

Unfortunately, she couldn't stay there. She was expected at her moonlighting job in half an hour. Hopefully, the weather would keep away all but the sickest patients, allowing her an opportunity to satisfy her curiosity.

She wore black slacks, a sweater, and a pair of Nikes, her

dark hair drawn back into a tight braid. Spread out on her sofa were a small Nikon automatic camera, two terrycloth hand towels, a pair of surgical gloves, an all-purpose Swiss Army knife, a tool kit, and a backpack. She packed the items together, added her cellular phone and a plastic poncho, and was ready.

Hefting her pack, she locked the back door of her apartment behind her, moving quickly down the stairs to the garage. She eased the car out to the street, its windshield wipers on high. The visibility was close to zero. She could barely make out the green traffic light at the corner as she made a cautious right turn and headed west to Santa Monica.

The rain was letting up as she passed the clinic and parked on the street a few feet beyond the parking lot. There were fewer cars than usual in the lot, no doubt a reflection of the miserable weather. She slipped out of the driver's seat, put on her backpack and poncho, and walked into the parking lot, heading for the back door.

From what she observed while working the first time, the door was left open for employees until the clinic was closed. It opened onto a short stretch of corridor at right angles to the main hallway, which contained the ladies' room. Alanna consulted her watch. She was right on time.

She reached the back door, stood under the overhang, dried her wet feet on the doormat, and removed the awkward poncho. The door opened silently onto an empty hallway. She walked inside, headed for the doctor's consult room, changed into her white coat, and left the backpack and poncho in the closet. Ready for work, she sauntered around the corner and cheerfully greeted the young women gossiping at the nurses' station.

As she had anticipated, the clinic was not crowded, and

the waiting room emptied rapidly. She filled her spare time catching up on charts at her desk. Ten minutes before closing, she told the staff she was leaving, hung up her white coat, and closed her office door with a bang. Just in case someone was paying attention, she also opened and closed the door to the parking lot before making a run for the bathroom, which was thankfully deserted.

Memorizing the position of the two toilet stalls, two sinks, and the mirror, she turned the bathroom light off, entered one of the stalls, and sat down to wait. Several deep breaths slowed her racing heartbeat and quieted her breathing.

A moment later, the door opened, and someone switched on the light. Alanna heard humming, then the sound of the adjacent stall door being opened. When the woman was finished, she flushed the toilet. Alanna held her breath.

"Are you coming?" Adelaide Hauptmann's voice called from the direction of the door.

Just a minute." Water ran in the sink. The light went off abruptly, and the door closed.

Alanna checked her watch, hoping Miss Hauptmann didn't have a full bladder. Nine ten. She'd wait until at least nine thirty before she made a move. It would probably be at least that long until everyone finished and went home.

It was a quarter to ten before she decided it was safe. She opened the stall and tiptoed to the bathroom door. The corridor was pitch black. She rummaged in her pack for her flashlight and turned it on low, using it to orient herself. Her steps were silent as she moved out the door.

There was no sound in the clinic. She felt her way along the wall to the bend in the hallway and paused again. Silence. She risked the flashlight. The first door to her left was the doctor's consultation room, the one beyond it contained the machine. Her fingers grasped the knob and turned. It was open.

The door squeaked as she slipped inside and closed it. She stood still, heart pounding. She looked around with the beam of the flashlight, relieved to see that the room had no windows. Placing her pack on the floor, she removed the towels she had brought and used them to seal the crack between the door and the floor. Satisfied, she flipped on the room light.

The device that haunted her was still there, its multi-jointed metal arms with their complex tips dangling. Alanna got to work. She retrieved her Nikon and photographed the device from all angles with particular attention to close-ups of the tips.

Completing her superficial survey, she extracted her toolkit and put on a pair of surgical gloves to avoid leaving fingerprints. A large metal plate was screwed onto the center of the device from which the arms emanated. Small engraved letters said "ARI, Menlo Park." The name was meaningless to her. She photographed the outside and selected a Phillips screwdriver. If she could remove the plate, she might be able to photograph the inside.

The inside was a maze of circuit boards and interconnecting wires. Alanna couldn't make heads or tails of it, but she knew someone who could. She removed the boards, one at a time, keeping them in order, taking photos of them as she went. She then replaced them and the metal cover. She hoped she hadn't made an error. If the device didn't work the next time it was needed, someone would be very angry.

Alanna replaced the tools in her pack and took a last look around. The room appeared exactly as she remembered when she entered. She shouldered her pack, turned off the lights, and exited, wiping the doorknob with a towel.

In a moment, she was at the back door. She was certain the clinic had a security alarm. No doubt it would go off the moment she exited. She prepared herself to sprint for her car as she twisted the knob. It didn't move.

Damn! She looked more carefully. It was one of those locks that locked from both sides. It locked you in as well as locking you out. She would need to find an alternate exit. Walking quickly down the hall, she headed for the waiting room. It was dark and cavernous, barely illuminated by the beam of her small flashlight. A red EXIT sign was in the far corner. She felt her way until she reached it. Another double lock. Another dead end.

A flash of panic began to rise from the pit of her stomach. Was she going to be trapped in here all night? There had to be another way. There must be a window somewhere. She turned down the hall, opening exam room after exam room. Not a window in sight. The whole back corridor was sealed in. That left only the front of the clinic. Perhaps one of the rooms near the nursing station.

A door behind the receptionist's desk opened into a spacious office. A nameplate on the desk said "Adelaide Hauptmann." There were drapes behind the desk. Closing the office door, Alanna pulled back the curtain, revealing a small window overlooking the adjacent alley. It was closed with a latch, but looked easy to open. If worst came to worst, she could knock out the glass using the drape to protect herself from cuts. She unfastened the latch, took a deep breath, and lifted the window frame.

The sound of the alarm took her breath away. Swinging her leg over the sill, she jumped to the ground and ran down the alley toward the parking lot. It was still raining, a fine drizzle that soaked her hair and ran down her neck. The ground was slick with puddles. She skidded, landed on her knee, forced herself up, and kept running. From the parking lot, the sound of the alarm was less strident. She had a few minutes before the security service appeared to investigate.

Gasping for breath, she opened her car door. She started the engine, relieved at its reliable purr, and drove with lights out and wipers on until she reached the corner. Then she continued north, barely breathing till she reached the safety of the lights and traffic on Montana Avenue.

61

February 11, 1996, 9:00 a.m.
Los Angeles, California

SHERMAN MAGNUSSEN POURED HIMSELF A second cup of coffee and turned to the obituary section of the Sunday paper. A small column noted the death of Lisa Keating, an obstetrician-gynecologist at Los Angeles Memorial Hospital. She was survived by her mother and stepfather, Dorothy and Henry Peterson of Dallas, Texas. Funeral services were scheduled for Monday at Greenbriar Cemetery. Magnussen made himself a mental note to have his secretary send a flower arrangement on behalf of the department.

"Sherman." Annabelle entered the dining room wearing a white silk dressing-gown and carrying the magazine section. She was fully made up and perfectly groomed as usual. Leaning over, she helped herself to a slice of toast, glancing, as she did, at her husband's reading material.

"Reading the obituaries, I see."

"Lisa Keating. I don't know what kind of world we live in

when young doctors are murdered in the streets. Such a waste of medical talent."

"I gather her talents were more than medical."

"I beg your pardon."

"Please, Sherman. Don't play ignorant with me. I know you were fucking her, and I know she was pregnant. All things considered, I'd say her death couldn't have come at a more convenient time for you. You do need to be more discreet."

"I thought I was being discreet."

Annabelle buttered her toast. "Look. I've never objected to your little extra-curricular activities as long as you've never objected to mine, but I will not be made a fool of. Do you know that your little slut had the nerve to come here and ask me to divorce you? Next time you have an affair, would you mind picking someone a little more mature, someone who doesn't want to have your baby? You're Chief of Gynecology, for God's sake. Haven't you ever heard of condoms?"

She reached over, grabbed the paper from him, and scanned the article. With a derisive snort, she tossed it across the table.

"Annabelle, I am sorry. I had no idea Lisa had been bothering you."

"Who else knows about this, Sherman?"

"No one. Lisa was hoping to persuade me to leave you. I told her it was out of the question and offered to pay for her abortion, but she wasn't the sort of girl who gave up easily. I don't imagine she would say anything to anyone until she was convinced there was no hope of getting what she wanted."

"And once she had given up?"

"Then she might have made an effort to embarrass me. It was an awkward situation."

"Well, you had better hope that she died with her mouth shut, Sherman, because if word gets out, I will have no choice but to play the wounded wife and file for divorce."

"I would hate for that to happen, my dear," Sherman said, finishing the last of his coffee. "Perhaps you're right. Lisa's death is a tragedy, but on balance, I don't think I shall miss her at all."

62

February 11, 1996, 11:00 a.m.
Dallas, Texas

THE ORGAN WAS PLAYING IN THE CHAPEL OF Greenbriar Cemetery in Dallas, Texas, as Brian Drew, attired in a somber black suit, marched down the aisle to seat himself in a pew behind Hank and Dorothy Peterson.

"Dorothy." Drew embraced his subordinate's tearful wife and patted Hank's shoulder. "I am so sorry. Lisa was such a special girl." Dorothy dabbed her eyes with a moist handkerchief.

Hank Peterson stood tall and poker-faced as he greeted family and friends. Few besides Drew would have noticed the lines of pain that crossed his face or would have realized the effort he was making to stay in control.

Poor bastard. He cared for the girl. Drew had always wondered if Hank had the hots for her. Must be hard on a man, living with such a nubile stepdaughter.

"Take some time off, Hank."

Hank started to shake his head.

"I insist."

The last thing Drew wanted was a grieving father around the office. More trouble than it was worth. Hank wouldn't be productive worth a damn for at least a week. He may as well use up his sick time. It was too sad about Lisa. Drew would miss her, and he'd have a hard time replacing her.

That reminded him. One of the last things he'd asked Lisa to do for him was to send him a list of the other residents with her assessment of how inclined they might be to feel favorable toward Health Web. He needed to take a careful look at it.

From what he recalled, two residents were moonlighting at the Santa Monica clinic. Perhaps he would start with them. He knew it was unlikely that he would find a sociopath as ingenious as Lisa a second time, but perhaps he could manage a garden-variety industrial spy.

63

———

February 11, 1996, 9:30 a.m.
Los Angeles, California

ALANNA WOKE LATER THAN USUAL ON SUNDAY morning after a fitful night's sleep filled with dreams of being chased through rainy streets by men with guns. Neither several days of rain nor the fall in the alley had been good for her joints, and she awakened stiff and in pain. She turned the shower on to maximum heat and stood under it, lathering herself head to toe, and breathing in the fragrant steam.

Her first errand this morning would be to drop off her film at the one-hour photo shop. Her second would be to treat herself to a latte and a chocolate croissant at the espresso bar down the street. Then she would figure out her next move.

It was one of those special mornings that followed a Los Angeles storm. The air was cool and crisp, the sky a perfect shade of blue. The Santa Monica Mountains, dotted with hillside homes, shone clear and bright in the morning air.

Alanna took a large bite of her croissant and sighed with pleasure.

Whoever said that you shouldn't eat chocolate for breakfast was deranged. Chocolate was the world's most perfect food. Combined with the right cup of coffee, it prodded your brain to new heights of creative energy.

She wanted to investigate one more thing. She had the feeling that something on the Health Web computer system was the key to everything she had sensed was not right about the clinic. How could she get into it? It was off-limits to the doctors, and she had no hacking skills. Perhaps she could access it as a patient.

Sunday was the perfect day to go to the urgent care center, pretending to be a patient. It was unlikely that Frau Hauptmann would be on duty on Sundays, and the weekend staff would be different from the weekday evening staff. She'd only been there twice. The chances of being recognized were slim.

With a grin, Alanna paid her bill, left a tip, and headed home with a quick stop at the nearest automatic teller machine to stock up on a supply of cash. If she visited the clinic under a false name, she couldn't use her credit card or a check. She was going to need a change of appearance.

Once inside her bedroom, she rummaged through her closet. She settled for faded jeans, a navy-blue T-shirt that had been washed too many times, and her oldest sneakers.

Washing her face clean of makeup, she brushed out her hair and let it hang loose down her back. A Dodger's cap and large sunglasses completed the look. As she stared at herself in the mirror, she decided she looked young, tired, and low on cash. Now all she needed was a new identity.

Her features weren't at all Hispanic, but thanks to the

multiethnic makeup of Los Angeles, she had other choices. Persian, Russian, or Armenian would be plausible.

Consulting the phone directory, she selected a name, address, and phone number for herself and scribbled them down. Grabbing an old purse she rarely used, Alanna left the house and headed for Santa Monica.

It was close to noon when she arrived. Several people were in the waiting room, but the clinic wasn't nearly as crowded as it had been the night she worked. She didn't recognize the receptionist.

"Can I help you?"

"Yes." Alanna paused. "I must see the doctor. I have pain in my back."

"Fill this out, please." The receptionist handed her a form on a clipboard.

Alanna took the form and sat down, printing MEHRI BABAKIAN with an address on Normandy. She handed it in.

"May I see your insurance card?"

"I don't have insurance. Will you take cash?"

"I think that will be fine, Miss Babakian. Have a seat. They'll call you in a few minutes."

While she waited, Alanna opened a copy of People magazine and updated herself on the romantic comings and goings of the Hollywood crowd. Finally, a young woman in a white nurse's uniform called her name.

"Follow me, please." She led her down the hall and into the big computer room.

"We need you to fill out some information about yourself."

"I don't type."

"You don't have to. Just point and click. I'll show you. Would you prefer English or Spanish?"

"English, please." Alanna sat while the girl turned on the console. A cheery Dr. John logo popped up. The girl typed Mehri Babakian's name, address, and phone number into the system. A list of questions appeared.

"All you have to do is read the question, put the arrow on 'yes' or 'no', and click. Like this." The nurse demonstrated.

Alanna pretended to catch on and filled in a detailed, fictional medical history for Mehri. The poor girl had every childhood disease known to man, along with pelvic inflammatory disease, ovarian cysts, bladder infections, and migraine headaches. She hadn't had any surgeries, however. Alanna didn't want to explain a missing surgical scar if someone examined her.

The next set of questions asked her to list her current symptoms. Alanna checked yes to back pain and pain while urinating. A picture of a back, divided into sections, asked her to select the place that hurt. She highlighted the right flank area, just over her right kidney. When she finished, the girl in the nurse's uniform selected print from the menu, and the computer spewed out several sheets of paper.

"What's that for?"

"That's your medical history for the doctor. Follow me, please." She took the sheets of paper out of the printer, glanced at them, and brought them to the nursing station. Then she opened a cupboard and handed Alanna a plastic cup.

"This is to collect some urine. The ladies' room is down the hall. Please follow the instructions posted on the wall to collect the specimen and bring it back to the station."

Alanna complied. She was anxious to look at the printout. If she couldn't manage it today, she would try to get hold of Mehri Babakian's chart the next time she worked here. She walked back to the nursing station, rubbing her side and wincing with pain, and handed her cup to the girl, who put it on the counter.

"Do I see the doctor now?"

"Come with me," the girl answered. She led Alanna down the hall to the room she had hoped for. The device stood there, just as she had left it the night before.

"What is that thing?"

"It's just a little machine the doctor uses to help examine you. Why don't you undress and change into this gown? I'll be back in a moment."

She left the room, leaving Alanna's chart in a holder on the door. Taking advantage of the nurse's absence, Alanna grabbed the chart and scanned the printout. It was a coherent narrative of the medical history she had input into the computer. Alanna had seen it before. What was new was the last page with the conclusions drawn from the history.

1-Rule out urinary tract infection
2-Rule out kidney infection
3-Rule out kidney stone

Plan
1-Urinanalysis and culture
2-Examination for kidney tenderness and fever
3-Trial of oral antibiotics if afebrile.
3-If not improved, IVP
4-If febrile to more than 101 degrees, evaluate for possible admission.

Alanna replaced the chart and quickly undressed. What a remarkable example, she thought, of cookbook medicine. The computer had it all figured out. A nurse practitioner wouldn't even have to think about it. Just follow the directions. The nurse reentered the room.

"Lie down flat, please," she said. "Put your arms down, over the side of the table."

"Will it hurt?"

"Not a bit."

"Do you like being a nurse? I used to think I wanted to be one."

"It's okay," the girl said. She was turning on the computer console, but Alanna couldn't read the screen from her position on the table.

"How many years did you have to go to school to do this?"

"Just a year after high school. I'm still in training. Open your mouth and say aah, please."

The arms of the device began to move. The first settled on her bare stomach. Another extruded a probe and placed it under her tongue. A third prodded her sharply in her right flank. Alanna jerked and groaned loudly. The prodding arm began to poke her stomach. She waited till it reached the vicinity of her bladder and flinched again.

"All done." The girl took the printout and Alanna's chart and headed toward the door.

"You can dress now."

"Don't I have to see the doctor first?"

"Doc's got all the information he needs. I'll be back in a minute with your prescriptions."

True to her word, the girl was back by the time Alanna had dressed with two printed prescriptions. One was for an antibiotic, the other for a bladder relaxant. Obviously, the computer had concluded she had a urinary tract infection rather than the kidney infection or stone she had been trying so hard to simulate. She wondered if they'd even bothered to look at the urine. Obviously, they'd chosen the low-cost solution first.

"You start these right away. Come back if you aren't better in twenty-four hours or if you get a fever."

The girl took her arm and guided her firmly to the check-out desk, where she was handed a bill for seventy-five dollars. Alanna paid in cash. The information was well worth the price.

Examination by a computer, under the control of an untrained high school graduate. She couldn't wait to get her photographs back and show them to the one person who could interpret them. As she replaced her wallet in her purse, the door behind the checkout station opened, and Adelaide Hauptmann strode out.

Hauptmann glanced at her and strode down the hall carrying a pile of charts. It was probably a good thing that Alanna hadn't made much of an impression on Miss Hauptmann at their first meeting.

Adelaide Hauptmann turned and stared at the pale young woman who had just walked out of the clinic. Such sloppy clothing. Her piggish nose wrinkled in distaste, and she frowned. Something about the woman was familiar. She had seen her before. She couldn't, at the moment, recall where. It would come back to her, though. Adelaide had a remarkable memory, and she never forgot a face.

64

─────────

February 12, 1996, 10:00 a.m.
Los Angeles, California

"G OD DAMN!" MURRAY THREW THE PAPER down on his desk and slammed his office door shut for good measure. Roth, who was sitting and waiting for him, winced.

"And good morning to you, too."

"It is not a good morning. If I find the son-of-a-bitch who leaked this information to the paper, I will personally pickle his balls in formaldehyde and feed them to him for breakfast."

"Lower your blood pressure, Murray. It was bound to come out eventually. How long did you think you could keep a serial killer under wraps? If he hadn't been killing bums and hookers, they'd have caught on to the story two weeks ago."

"I suppose, only now I've got all the brass breathing down my neck wanting a break in the case. I'm doing every-thing I can. I've even got a good suspect, but I can't arrest him yet without a shred of forensic evidence to link him to any of these killings. The defense attorney would kick my ass all over the criminal court building."

"You mean Magnussen?"

"Of course, I mean fucking Magnussen. In Keating's case, he had motive and means. The question is, did he have opportunity, and, if so, what was his motive for bumping off all the others? And how does all this tie into Health Web? There's gotta be a connection.

"The other questions are, where did he do it, and why did he botch them? He couldn't have killed them in the hospital operating room and carried the dead bodies to his Mercedes in the doctor's parking lot. The guy's got to have a hiding place, and we have to find it."

"I've run him through all the databases," Roth said. "No record. Not even a parking ticket, unless there's something sealed and juvenile."

"What about court records? Has the guy ever been sued?"

"A couple of malpractice cases. Mostly due to resident incompetence. His name is always on the chart, so he always gets named. He's never had a judgment against him."

"Real estate?"

"He owns an estate in lower Bel Air and a little summer cottage in Vail. He's married to Annabelle Cunningham of The Cunninghams."

"You mean Cunningham Oil, Cunningham Shipping, the Cunningham hotel chain? Those Cunninghams?"

"You got it," Roth said. "Broad's loaded. If Lisa Keating threatened to interfere with his happy marriage, I imagine he'd stand to lose a small fortune."

"Any indication he had a little love nest?"

"Not so far, but we're working on it. Top priority. We've also got his vitae. We've got guys checking every place he ever worked or went to school to see if there's any harassment history or any similar crimes in the places he lived when he was there."

"Okay. I can't think of anything else. Keep at it. I have a meeting this afternoon with the chief. He'll probably read me the riot act. What!"

Murray pressed the speaker phone and silenced the buzz of the intercom.

"Phone for you, sir. It's a Dr. Alanna Davidson. She says you interviewed her at the hospital."

Murray pressed the receiver to his ear. "Mosher here. What can I do for you, Doctor?"

"Detective, thanks for taking my call. I was wondering if we could talk sometime today. I read the article in today's paper, and I have reason to suspect that the person you're looking for may work here at Memorial. It's a long story."

"Can you come down here?"

"I've got a clinic all afternoon, and then I have to go home and pack. I'm taking a late flight to Washington. Is there any possibility you could come to my apartment around six?"

"I'll be there," Murray said. "Give me the address."

He wrote it down and glanced at Roth as he hung up the phone.

"She thinks the killer may be someone at Memorial. She'll tell me about it tonight. Cross your fingers. We need a break in this case, and I hope to hell Alanna Davidson is it."

65

———

February 12, 1996, 6:00 p.m.
Los Angeles, California

A T PROMPTLY SIX IN THE EVENING, MURRAY rang the bell of Alanna Davidson's apartment. She greeted him with a smile and motioned for him to take a seat in a comfortable armchair. She was dressed in jeans and a simple white T-shirt. Her shiny, dark hair swung loose, and she was without makeup. Once again, Murray was struck by her resemblance to his daughter Michelle.

The couch was covered with a pile of clothes and books, which Alanna was packing into a small suitcase. The scent of pizza permeated the apartment, reminding Murray that he hadn't had a chance to have supper.

"Please help yourself," she said, waving toward the small kitchen. There's Coke in the refrigerator. I'm about to face a week's worth of my mother's healthy, low-fat meals, so I figured I'd better stock up on junk food while I can."

Murray couldn't help himself. He started to laugh, heaved himself out of the chair, and took her up on her offer. The pizza was pepperoni, and he cut himself two slices. Carrying the plate and a cold drink back to the living room, he settled himself comfortably and waited for her to talk.

Alanna folded the last of her clothing and zipped the suitcase. She seated herself beside it on the sofa, kicking off her shoes.

"I hope I don't wind up wasting your time, detective, but I read the article in this morning's paper about the serial killer. I have reason to suspect that something is going on at Memorial that might be connected, and I decided to tell you about it, even if I do wind up making a fool of myself."

She began with the death of Belinda Lancaster and described Larry Rosen's pathology findings and her search for the responsible sample of amniotic fluid. Then she told him about Suzanne Saunders and Arthur Underwood.

"At first, I suspected that Lisa Keating herself could have been responsible for everything. She had access to the amniotic fluid sample and the medical knowledge to use it on Belinda. She could easily have gotten hold of extra morphine, and could also have gotten into the pharmacy and switched the antibiotics when the pharmacist was working on the patient floor. She was the only resident on call all three nights. I checked the nurse and pharmacist schedule as well."

"What motive would she have had?" Murray asked.

"I'm not sure. I know that a company called Health Web is trying to buy the hospital. Belinda's husband, Suzanne Saunders, and Arthur Underwood were all on the hospital board and against the buyout. Those deaths would certainly have tipped the balance in favor of Health Web."

"I can't imagine why Lisa Keating would have cared enough, one way or the other. Then, I thought, perhaps the killer you called The Surgeon was at Memorial, and Lisa had somehow found out about him. Maybe he killed Lisa because she knew too much."

Murray set his plate aside and wiped tomato sauce off his hands and mouth with a paper napkin.

"That's quite a story. Why didn't you tell me when I interviewed you at the hospital? Withholding information from the police can get you into a lot of trouble."

Alanna flushed. "It wasn't information. It's a lot of suspicion and conjecture that may lead nowhere. I don't suppose you have any information to add that would be helpful?"

"If I did, I couldn't tell you. The information flow goes only one way. Do you have any idea of who The Surgeon could be?"

"Believe me, I'd tell you if I did. The person who killed Belinda had to be very medically sophisticated. If I were guessing, I'd look for a doctor. The thought that one of my colleagues could be a mass murderer is not very reassuring."

"If Lisa was killed because she knew too much, you'd better stop investigating, or you could be next. Promise me, you'll keep quiet. Anything else you want to tell me?"

"I had one other thought. Did you know that Lisa Keating had a locker in the second-floor women's locker room? I don't know if you searched it, but maybe she found evidence of something and put it there. It's the only secure place we residents have in the hospital. I'd look if you haven't already."

Murray nodded. "We didn't know, and we will look. Thank you." He got up from the armchair and faced her.

"If you think of anything else, please call me." He took out one of his cards and wrote a number on the back. "If it's urgent, you can page me by calling this number. I'm glad you're going out of town. If your suspicions have any foundation, you could be in danger."

He put a hand gently on her shoulder. "Be careful, Doctor, and thank you. You've given me a lot to think about."

Murray left the apartment, closing the door firmly behind him. It was seven o'clock and he had his evening's work cut out for him. Now, more than ever, he was convinced that Sherman Magnusen was his best suspect for The Surgeon.

66

February 12, 1996, 7:30 p.m.
Los Angeles, California

AFTER LEAVING ALANNA'S APARTMENT, Mosher paged Roger Roth, and the two drove to the hospital to interview Larry Rosen. The pathologist confirmed Alanna's story. He took the two men to his lab, where he showed them the slides and the DNA testing results. Mosher confiscated the material and the sample tube from which the fluid had come. It was doubtful that it contained useful fingerprints, but worth a try.

Their next call was to the County morgue, where they found out who had performed Suzanne Saunders' autopsy. They spoke to him and obtained two helpful pieces of information. The first was that Suzanne had died of a huge morphine overdose. The second was that the syringe found in the wastepaper basket in her room contained no fingerprints. The medical examiner was puzzled, since he would have expected Suzanne's thumbprint on the plunger if the dose had been self-administered.

The two men refrained from calling Arthur Underwood. It was late, and they decided that part of the investigation could wait until morning.

At eight-thirty a.m., Murray, hair still damp from his shower, sat at his desk at the Robbery Homicide Division reviewing the morning's reports.

"You had a call from Dallas PD," one of the secretaries said, placing a message slip on his desk. "They said Lisa Keating's calls to Health Web were all for Brian Drew. He's the CEO. If you have any questions, you can call them."

"Interesting." Murray stared at the paper.

"What's interesting?" Roth said, putting his cup of herbal tea on Murray's desk.

"It seems like Lisa Keating was buddy-buddy with the head honcho at Health Web. Let's see if we can get phone files for the corporate offices and their home numbers. I'd like to know how often the two talked, and when."

"I'll get someone on it. What's on the agenda for today?"

"We search that locker, and we talk to the hospital president. Then we come back here and see how many ways we can get the pieces to fit before we bring in Magnussen for another interview."

67

February 12, 1996, 10:00 a.m.
Los Angeles, California

M osher put the contents of Lisa Keating's locker in an evidence bag and handed the copies of her bankbook and appointment calendar to Roth.

"Get over there and check out those $3000 deposits and the $10,000 ones. I want to know where she got her money. Get a warrant if anyone at the bank gives you any trouble."

"Don't have a stroke," Roth said. "I know what to do. I'll page you as soon as I find something."

"Did you notice those initials, SM, all over her date book? I bet they stand for Sherman Magnussen, and she had a date with him on the day of her death."

Murray left the locker room and took the hospital elevator to the top floor and Arthur Underwood's office. His secretary showed Murray right in.

Underwood rose from his desk and shook Murray's hand. "Please take a seat, Detective, and tell me how I can help you. All of us at Memorial were deeply distressed at Dr. Keating's death."

"I have a few questions. I'm not sure yet how they are related to the murder, but I'd appreciate any information you can give me. I understand that Health Web offered to purchase Los Angeles Memorial Hospital. What is the status of that offer? Who makes the decision, and when?"

Underwood sighed. "That's a little complicated right now. The hospital Board of Directors was supposed to have voted on it this month. There are five board members: myself, the Chief of the Medical Staff, Dr. Swerdlow, Colin Lancaster, the late Suzanne Saunders, and Neville Harte, the CEO of Harte Industries. If you'd asked me a few weeks ago, I'd have been confident that the Board would turn down Health Web's offer.

"Miss Saunders, Dr. Swerdlow, and I were all opposed. Mr. Harte was in favor, but we had the majority. As you know, Miss Saunders died just recently, and Mr. Lancaster is suing the hospital because his wife died in childbirth. I'm in the process of taking legal steps to remove him from the Board based on a profound conflict of interest. At the moment, we don't have a quorum, and we can't vote on anything."

"How will you replace them?" Murray asked.

"We're seeking possible candidates now to replace Miss Saunders, but we can't replace Lancaster until the legal situation is clarified."

"Did it ever strike you, Dr. Underwood, as more than a coincidence that two deaths involving board members or their families, and your near miss, all occurred at exactly the right time to interfere with the vote on Health Web?"

Underwood stared at him, appalled at the implication, his fair complexion turning ruddy.

"Detective, are you implying that someone has been committing murder to influence this acquisition? That's absurd. Believe me, I looked into these incidents very carefully. I certainly have no suspicion of foul play."

"Did you know Dr. Keating?" Murray asked, switching the subject before Underwood could become any more agitated.

"Not personally. I can't possibly know all the residents at this institution."

"Would it surprise you to learn that her stepfather is a Vice President at Health Web?"

"I wasn't aware of that, but I can hardly see what difference it makes who her father was. She was murdered by a serial killer."

"We believe so. I don't like coincidences, and this case is developing too many for my taste. I appreciate your time."

He rose from his chair, shook Underwood's hand again, and took his leave. As he headed for the parking lot, his pager beeped.

"It's me, Roth. All the deposits were cash. Untraceable. I called her folks in Texas. They deny sending her any supplementary income. Mrs. Peterson said that Lisa managed just fine on her salary. One more thing. We've found Magnussen's hiding place. He's got a little apartment all to himself in Westwood. Should I get a search warrant?"

"You bet," Murray said. "Call me as soon as you've got it. We'll search the place first and then bring him in."

68

February 13, 1996, 2:00 p.m.
Los Angeles, California

Adelaide Hauptmann, the manager of the Health Web Clinic, was feeling irritable. It was not like her to forget a face, and she knew she'd seen that sloppily dressed woman before. She asked the receptionist for the name, thinking it would jog her memory, but Mehri Babakian meant nothing to her. She'd let it go for a while, figuring that it would come to her eventually as it always did, but two days later, she was still without an answer. Nor did she know why it was bothering her so much.

Adelaide, however, relied on her instincts. If something gnawed at her, it would probably prove to be important. Picking up her phone, she buzzed the receptionist.

"Bring me the chart on Mehri Babakian, would you?"

The receptionist complied, entering Adelaide's office a few moments later with a slim manila file folder. Adelaide scanned it. Mehri lived on Normandy Avenue, was single, and had no insurance. She had been complaining of abdominal and back pain and had been treated as a presumptive urinary tract infection. The urine analysis, however, had come back normal.

Miss Babakian had filled out a whole history on the Dr. John protocol and had been examined by the auto-examiner. The computer had suggested several other possible diagnoses but had, as it had been programmed to do, treated the cheapest thing first, figuring that if Mehri wasn't better, she'd be back some other time. Adelaide decided to call and see how Mehri was. She dialed the home number on the registration slip.

"Seven-Eleven, can I help you?"

"May I speak to Mehri Babakian, please?"

"Sorry. No one by that name works here."

So, Mehri Babakian gave a fake phone number. Had the name and address been fake as well? Adelaide picked up the phone again.

"I have a job for you," she said to the person who answered. "I want you to go to this address. Find out if a Mehri Babakian lives there. Tall, Middle Eastern features, dark hair."

Adelaide buzzed the front desk again. "Is Ellen working today? Tell her to come in here, please."

Ellen was the young technician who had worked with Mehri Babakian. After a timid knock, the girl opened Adelaide's door.

"Sit down," Adelaide said. She handed her the manila folder. "Do you happen to remember this woman? She was seen on Sunday morning."

Ellen looked at the chart. "The one with the urine infection?"

Adelaide nodded. "Do you remember anything unusual about her?"

Ellen's brow wrinkled. "Not really. She was friendly. Asked me lots of questions about what it was like to be a nurse."

"What questions exactly?"

"Oh, how I liked it, how many years I'd gone to school, that kind of thing. She wanted to know when she would get to see the doctor."

"Did she seem interested in our computer setup?"

"Yeah, I guess so. She asked me what the thing with all the arms was for."

"And what did you tell her?"

"Same as I tell all the patients. It's a little machine the doctor uses to help examine you."

Adelaide chewed on a pencil, tapping her fingers on the wooden desktop. "Was she left alone, by any chance?"

"Just for a few minutes while I brought the papers out to the front."

"Interesting." Adelaide took the pencil out of her mouth. "You can go now," she said.

As Ellen opened the door, the receptionist came in.

"Miss Hauptmann, Dr. Washington just called. He wanted to let you know that he'll be covering the evening shift tomorrow afternoon. Dr. Davidson's out of town."

"Very well. Not a problem so long as the shift is covered." Adelaide leaned back in her chair, and then it came to her. Put on some makeup and decent clothes, and Mehri Babakian was a dead ringer for Alanna Davidson. She should have seen it sooner. That Dr. Davidson, who was so interested in the computer room, the one with all the questions. Adelaide had taken an immediate dislike to her.

An hour later, she received the information she'd been waiting for.

"That address you gave me belongs to a gas station," the man said. "There's no Mehri Babakian there."

Adelaide hung up the phone. Mehri Babakian was a complete fabrication. Unless Adelaide's eagle eyes had failed her, Mehri and Alanna Davidson were the same. Maybe she was a spy from some other medical corporation. Industrial espionage was everywhere, and some of the other HMOs would give their eye teeth to get hold of Doctor John.

Adelaide reached for her phone and dialed a number in Dallas, Texas.

69

———

February 13, 1996, 3:00 p.m.
Los Angeles, California

B RIAN DREW ALWAYS THOUGHT ADELAIDE Hauptmann
would have been a far better and more ruthless CEO
for ARI than her brother. Adelaide was not a stupid woman.
He trusted her with the delicate task of overseeing the trials
on Doctor John, and she had done a superb job of creating
just the setting Drew had envisioned for all the Health Web
clinics. Adelaide shared his vision.

Huge profits were to be made by automating health care
for the increasingly large aging population and by controlling or eliminating the physicians who had, for too long,
controlled the financial pie. Drew estimated it would take
only a few more months to iron out the final bugs in the
system, equip all his hospitals and clinics, and use the
profits generated to control an ever-increasing share of the
healthcare delivery system.

It was crucial that none of his competitors get hold of his
system until he was so far ahead it wouldn't matter. Then he

could increase his profits even further by selling Dr. John at an exorbitant price.

They had been careful to keep the system under wraps. None of the clinic employees, except for Adelaide and the physicians, had either the intelligence or the sophistication to understand what he had created, and they had been careful to keep the doctors away from the system.

Adelaide's suspicion of Alanna Davidson disturbed him greatly. If he had used a physician for espionage, there was no reason why the idea might not occur to one of his competitors. He had never known Adelaide to disturb him with anything frivolous or incorrect.

Drew had made up his mind. First, he would find out everything he could about this resident, and then he would do whatever it took to stop her.

70

———

February 14, 1996, 6:00 a.m.
Washington, DC

S NOW WAS FALLING LAZILY TO THE RUNWAY, piling itself into gentle drifts as Alanna's plane taxied to its gate, moments ahead of what promised to be a major blizzard. If she'd waited for the morning flight, Dulles airport would have been closed, and she would have been diverted to New York or Philadelphia. Alanna reached into the overhead bin and pulled out her small suitcase. Thank goodness she'd listened to her mother this time and brought a few warm things.

Miriam was waiting for her at the gate, her slim figure fashionably dressed in beige wool slacks and a matching hooded parka with a fur lining. Her face lit up with a smile as she spotted her daughter and greeted her with a huge hug. Alanna smelled the familiar scent of freesia, her mother's favorite cologne, and pulled back to look at her.

Miriam's hair, once as dark as Alanna's, had turned a fashionable gray, and she had cut it to a thick short bob that flattered her face. The eyes were identical to Alanna's except for the fine lines and baggy skin that proclaimed her sixty-four years.

"You look beautiful, darling," Miriam said, hooking her arm into Alanna's. "You must be freezing in that jacket."

"Thanks for reminding me. I need to get some clothes out of here."

She perched her suitcase on a chair and retrieved a thick, wine-colored sweater and a black windbreaker. "That should do until I get home and raid my closet. I'm sure there's a winter coat in there somewhere."

"Do we need to go to baggage claim?"

Alanna shook her head. She turned her small suitcase on end to wheel it, and the two women followed the signs to the parking garage.

Miriam's car was a dark gray, ten-year-old Lincoln Continental in perfect condition. Alanna slid into the passenger seat, inhaling the familiar smell of leather, and fastened her seat belt. Her mother reached for the controls and turned on the heat and the rear window defroster.

Miriam guided the car out of the lot, flicking on the wipers as they exited. Traffic was moving slowly, the streets covered with snow, rapidly converting to ice. She eased the vehicle onto the beltway and headed toward the city.

"So, are you going to keep me in suspense, or are you going to tell me your news?"

"It's a long story, Mom. I'd prefer to tell it just once, and I'd like to wait until both you and Dad can listen simultaneously. How is Dad these days?"

"The usual. Depressed, bitter, angry, cranky, and in general, impossible to live with. Other than that, his health is as good as can be expected for a paraplegic." She turned the car onto the Beltway, positioning herself for their exit.

"How is he spending his time? Have you been able to interest him in anything?"

Miriam sighed. "Your father's favorite activities used to be sex, golf, tennis, and skiing, not necessarily in that order. Since he can't indulge in any of them from a wheelchair, he's spending most of his time obsessing about the stupidity of the FBI, the incompetence of the Arlington police, and the loss of his precious robot. Suffice it to say that he is not a joy to be around."

The tears that sprang to her eyes belied the sharp sarcasm of her tone. Alanna knew that Miriam adored her husband, and her inability to make him feel better gnawed at her constantly.

The car pulled up in front of their Georgetown house, a parking spot still miraculously available. Miriam shut the engine and put on the parking brake.

As the front door opened, the Davidsons' elderly Scottish Terrier, Mac, greeted Alanna, his stubby tail wagging frantically back and forth. Mac was too dignified to bark and too arthritic to jump, but he followed her loyally into the house, sniffing at the leg of her jeans.

Alanna bent down and scratched behind his graying ears. He'd been a puppy when she first got him, and she'd missed him terribly when she went to college. She considered getting another dog. Now she was glad she hadn't. An apartment was no place for an animal, and with her hours, a dog would be terribly lonely.

"Tired, darling? Did you get any sleep on the plane?"

"Not much." Alanna yawned. "I've never been very good at sleeping sitting up. I could use a nap. Is Dad up?"

"I don't think so. He went to bed rather late last night, and he sleeps in until at least ten these days. Why don't you go to your room and rest a little? When you wake up, we can all have breakfast, and you can tell us the reason for this surprise visit."

"Good idea. Is Sammy home?"

Miriam glanced in the direction of the stairs. "He was when I left. You might want to get some sleep before you see him."

Alanna evaluated her mother's expression. "Is he off his medications again?"

"He hates the way Haldol makes him feel." She shrugged, with a look that said she was helpless. Alanna restrained herself from commenting. If she wasn't home to help with Sam, she could hardly criticize.

71

February 14, 1996, 7:45 a.m.
Washington, DC

A FTER GIVING MIRIAM A QUICK HUG, ALANNA wheeled
her suitcase up the dark wood stairs, carpeted with a
blue oriental runner. The upstairs banister had been
removed to make space for the unsightly metal elevator that
allowed her father to descend in his wheelchair to the
ground floor. At the top of the stairs, Alanna walked into her
childhood bedroom.

The room smelled fresh and welcoming. The drapes had
been drawn, and the blinds opened to allow sunshine to
spill onto the four-poster bed with its yellow chintz canopy
and spread. The plush carpet welcomed her tired feet.

She removed her coat and hung it in her half-empty
closet. The old Stickley rocker with its plump, cushioned
seat stood next to the bed. She lowered herself into it and
perused the bookshelves. Her college texts had been
moved to the lower shelves, and her mother, an insatiable
reader, had filled the upper ones with novels. Many of

them were ones Alanna had wanted to read but hadn't had time for.

Alanna kicked off her shoes, closed her eyes, and rocked gently. It felt good to be home, good and safe. If she wasn't careful, she'd be tempted to spend her time curled up in bed reading instead of trying to solve the mystery that brought her here.

"Hey, Lanna. You're just in time to see my latest opus."

She looked up. Her older brother Samuel, her parents' pride, joy, and deepest disappointment, stood in the doorway. She could tell he'd been off his meds for a while. His dark curly hair was uncut and unkempt, his chin unshaven. He was wearing torn jeans and a t-shirt stained with paint, and his hands and nails were covered in multi-hued acrylics.

"Hey, Sammy," she forced a smile. "What're you up to?"

"Just finished a painting. The Smithsonian offered me a bundle for it, but I haven't decided if I should let them have it or send it to the Louvre. It's important to get the right exposure for the world to appreciate your art."

"I bet it is. What's the painting of?"

He motioned her to follow him. "I'm glad I'm finally getting a chance to finish this thing. It's been hard, what with the President constantly calling me to supervise the White House art collection."

"I can imagine."

"You know the Republicans tried to arrest me last week. They sent the FBI to the house, but I had a warning."

"Your voices tell you?""

"Shh. Don't talk about them. The house is probably bugged. Newt Gingrich is planning to collect all the art in Washington and drown it in the Potomac."

Alanna repressed a laugh. "I didn't know you could

paint," she said, trying to change the subject as she followed him down the hall.

"I'm leaving for Moscow tomorrow. There's a man there who wants to explode a nuclear weapon on the Golden Gate Bridge, and the government needs me to investigate."

"Then we'd better look at the paintings before you leave."

Samuel's room was filthy, smelly, and filled with huge canvases. They were abstracts, in rich dark colors with occasional slashes of crimson or bright purple. Alanna held her breath, examining them slowly, one after the other. They were powerful, disturbing, and undeniably brilliant. She circled the room, finally returning to her brother, who stood waiting, arms folded across his chest. Perhaps the link people speculated about between madness and creativity was true.

"Sammy, do you have any idea how good these are?"

His face broke into a smile at her praise.

"You know," he confided in a whisper, "they've commissioned a new one for the Getty Museum in Los Angeles."

"I'm so proud of you."

"Really?"

"Really." She walked over and hugged him tightly, burying her head against his chest so he couldn't see her tears.

72

February 14, 1996, 10:00 a.m.
Washington, DC

ALANNA MANAGED A SHORT NAP AND AWOKE TO the aroma of fresh coffee. She showered, put on a warm terry robe, and descended to the kitchen. The wheelchair elevator was on the ground floor, and her parents were seated at the kitchen table, mugs and morning paper in hand.

Avram's eyes lit up when he saw her, and he opened his arms. "How's my girl?"

She bent and hugged him tight, blinking to control the tears that always seemed her first reaction to seeing him. All her life, she had viewed him as a giant, but since the shooting, he'd become thin and frail, his normally tanned face pale, his cheeks sunken. He'd let his curly gray hair grow untidily over his neck and ears. Only his green eyes with their formidable black eyebrows appeared alive.

"I'm starving and happy to be home. I've missed you guys."

"Well, I can do something about the starving part," Miriam said. "How about a cheese omelet and a toasted bagel?"

"Perfect," Alanna sat, facing her father, noticing the slim hands resting on the plaid wool blanket that covered his knees and the unsightly urinary catheter that he found so humiliating. "Have you two eaten?"

"We have," Avram said. "We've been sitting here speculating about the reason for your surprise visit."

"I'll tell you in a minute, but tell me first about Sam. I saw the paintings. They're incredible."

"I know," Miriam said. "He says the Haldol makes his hands shake and takes away his voices. It's the voices that tell him what to paint. He stopped it six months ago, and he keeps getting worse."

"He can't string two sentences together that make any sense," Avram said. "When he's on the drug, he sounds rational and can't concentrate on anything for more than a few minutes. He'll never be right, no matter what we do."

Alanna could hear the grief and the anger in her father's voice, and it exacerbated the guilt she always felt and tried so hard to push away. Guilt for being the normal one, for being in Los Angeles while her parents coped at home.

"Do you know anyone in the art world?" Alanna asked. "Anyone who could help get his art shown?"

Miriam smiled. "I've thought of that."

"Waste of time," Avram said. "What would you do if they want to meet the artist? Even if people like his work, he won't continue to produce it. Remember his great novel? Five hundred pages of incoherent gibberish."

"That was different," Miriam said. "You've refused to look, but he's finished a dozen pieces, and they're wonderful. He's a brilliant painter."

"He was a brilliant medical student," Avram said, "before his nervous breakdown. Brilliance isn't the issue, is it?"

Miriam sighed and poured three cups of coffee. It was clear they'd had this conversation before.

"I still think we should try to get his work shown. He may be schizophrenic, but that doesn't mean that praise and recognition won't make him feel good. He deserves to have something positive in his life," Alanna said.

"I agree," said Miriam, "and I do know some people."

"That's great, Mom." Alanna reached into her pocket and took out the packet of photos.

"Maybe we should talk more about Sam a little later. Why don't you let me tell you why I'm home? It's a complicated story.

"A few weeks ago, I started a new moonlighting job at a clinic run by Health Web. They're a big medical conglomerate that owns many hospitals, nursing homes, clinics, medical supply companies, and physician practices. Corporate medicine at its greediest. They're making a major effort to purchase Los Angeles Memorial.

"My first night there, I noticed something odd about the clinic. There were a huge number of patients, but I saw only a small fraction of them. The rest of the clinic staff consisted of people who looked too young and seemed too uneducated to be licensed PAs or nurse practitioners. I accidentally wandered into a room I wasn't supposed to be in and found this."

She passed the packet over to Avram. He looked at the photos, his brows creasing, first in curiosity, then in outrage.

"Where did they get this?" he demanded.

"Am I right, Dad? The moment I saw it, I thought it was ELECTRA. The tips of the arms looked different, but everything else seemed the same."

"How did you get all the pictures, Alanna? I find it hard to believe they'd let you take it apart."

"Better you shouldn't know," she said, laughing. "You wouldn't approve, and I can assure you, they have no idea I have them."

"I know these circuits as well as your mother's face. I spent years designing them. What else do you know about this thing?"

Miriam placed a hot plate in front of Alanna and reached over to take the photos from her husband's hands. She scanned them thoughtfully.

"What's this ARI?" she asked.

"I don't know. I assume it's the name of the company that manufactured it. ARI, Menlo Park. It was stamped on the cover plate. I thought Dad might know."

"I don't, but I'm going to find out. Are they operating with this?"

"Not as far as I can tell. They seem to be using it to examine patients. They have a whole computer system they call Doctor John. It takes the patient's complete history. Then the patient lies down, and the robot listens, takes photos, and palpates. It's like having a physical exam by a machine. The computer evaluates the data, comes up with a list of diagnoses, and a treatment plan. The technicians follow the instructions."

"Is it any good?" Miriam asked.

"It has its limits," Alanna said. "I walked in last Sunday morning, in the guise of a patient. I was mimicking a kidney stone, and I got treated for a urinary tract infection. Either my performance was inadequate, or the thing is programmed to treat the disease requiring the fewest tests first."

"Did you see a doctor?" said Avram.

"No. That's the whole point. They seem to be using your robot as a physician replacement. That's how they can run a huge clinic with one moonlighting resident physician and lots of cheap, completely untrained help. The only patients I saw the night I worked, were so sick that they needed to be hospitalized."

Avram wheeled himself back from the table and swiveled his chair to reach the kitchen wall phone.

"Bradley Trayner, please." He waited as the connection was placed. "Brad, Avram Davidson here. I need some information. A company called ARI out of Menlo Park. I want everything your brokerage firm can get on it. Financial statements, board of directors, subsidiaries, stock performance, names and resumes of the CEO and all the operating officers, all the products, major customers."

Avram laughed. "No, I don't have any inside information and I'm not buying stock—yet. Fax it to me at home ASAP, will you? Thanks."

He turned to his wife and daughter. "Well, I found out one thing. ARI stands for American Robotics Institute. Trayner thought I knew something he didn't. Got all excited. He'll probably have the material to me by the time you finish your breakfast. I'll get to the bottom of this if it's the last thing I do. I'll be in my study, waiting for that fax."

Miriam gave Alanna a long look as her husband wheeled himself down the hall.

"Well, I haven't seen him so animated since before the shooting. I'm not sure if I like this or not, Alanna. What if he can't get to the bottom of it? He'll feel even more depressed than he does already."

"Mom, he can't be any worse than he is, and this is the

first clue we've had in four years. How could I have not told him?"

Miriam reached across the table for Alanna's hand. "I know, sweetheart. I hope the two of you haven't gotten into something you can't handle."

73

February 14, 1996, 11:30 a.m.
Washington, DC

AVRAM'S STUDY WAS ALANNA'S FAVORITE ROOM in the house. French doors opened into a small but interesting garden, and floor-to-ceiling bookshelves reflected her father's eclectic tastes, with books on every subject from medicine and politics to electrical engineering. Two comfortable wing chairs were arranged in front of an elaborate marble fireplace, and Avram's huge mahogany desk with its computer and fax was now rearranged for easy access with his wheelchair. Alanna settled down on one of the chairs.

"Do you have a theory about all this, Dad?"

"I've always had a theory. The problem is that no one was interested in it. Those smartasses at the FBI thought a medical robot wasn't worth their time. If it wasn't a military weapon that was stolen, why bother? By the time I got out of the intensive care unit and was well enough to start asking questions, they'd closed their investigation and had moved on to other things."

"What did they find?"

"I'll tell you what they told me. I have no idea if it's the truth or not. They said there was no forced entry to the building, my suite, or my private office. The guard was poisoned with a huge dose of barbiturates, apparently administered along with caffeine. It appeared as if he let his killers willingly into the building and shared a friendly cup of coffee with them.

"They had security cards, or they couldn't have gotten into the place, and mine were stolen when I was shot. They were able to access the computer system and download all the software. Either they were superb hackers, or someone gave them the password. I think it was an inside job. They knew exactly what they were looking for and where to find me."

"Who knew the password besides you?"

"The whole software team. We had at least ten guys working on it."

"Did anyone else have the key to your office?"

"I think the security office keeps key cards to everything locked away, but no one else on my team had the card to my private office."

"You think you were shot to obtain that key? Why couldn't they have just downloaded everything from one of the other workstations? Why did they have to get into your office?"

"Good question. I think they wanted all the backup discs. They wiped the hard disc to destroy the software, and they stole all the backups. I think whoever was behind this wanted to make sure it would be as difficult as possible to restart the project. I don't know if the same guys who shot me also took Electra, but I'm positive there's a connection."

"Didn't the FBI come up with any clues to the break-in?"

"Again, I'm not privy to the investigation. They'd have been fools not to have looked into everyone on the team, but no one was arrested, so I have to assume they hit a dead end."

A log broke in the fireplace, sending a shower of sparks up toward the chimney. At the same moment, the fax began generating paper. Avram grabbed the sheets and began to read.

"American Robotics Institute is a small company started by Howard Hauptmann twenty years ago. It manufactures robots used for assembly line work primarily in the auto industry. It was privately held until four years ago, when it was purchased by Health Web."

"You're kidding?" Alanna held out her hand for the printout. "The person who runs the Health Web clinic is Adelaide Hauptmann. That can't be a coincidence."

"Let's look at their financial statement."

"You look at their financial statement. I wouldn't have a clue. Give me something else to read."

Avram handed her the last few sheets of paper, and the two read quietly for several minutes.

"According to these," the Colonel said, "it looks like they've taken most of the profits and put them into research and development. What have you got?"

"Just a list of their key employees. Any of these names look familiar?"

She handed the list to her father.

"You bet. We may have found our Judas. Their head of research and development is Walter McGreavy, the former head of my software team."

74

—————

February 14, 1996, 7:30 p.m.
Washington, DC

MIRIAM DAVIDSON SPENT THE AFTERNOON IN the kitchen, cooking an elaborate dinner which Alanna, Sam, and Avram ate with gusto. After dinner, Sam drifted upstairs, and the rest of them retreated to the den with coffee and cake, deciding what to do next.

"There are three possible scenarios, as I see it," Avram said. "Either Walter McGreavy came up with the idea of stealing the system and approached American Robotics or Health Web, or one of the two companies found out about it and recruited him."

"My money is on Health Web," Alanna said. "It stands to gain the most from using the system, and it acquired American Robotics after Electra was stolen. They probably needed someone with robotics expertise to modify it for their own needs."

"Tell me about McGreavy," Miriam asked. "Why would he do something like this?"

"McGreavy was a career army officer and a brilliant programmer," Avram said. "About a year after the robot was stolen, he resigned his commission and went into private industry. So did several other members of the team. DARPA had decided by then that they wouldn't fund the effort to rebuild the system. As to why, the only answers I can come up with are greed and ego. I'm sure American Robotics is paying him a lot more than the government was."

"Still," Miriam said, "to attempt the murder of his superior officer. He must have hated you."

Avram shrugged and sipped his black coffee. "I don't know that hate had anything to do with it. I'm sure he didn't pull the trigger. McGreavy may not even have known someone was going to shoot me. He may have gotten involved with people who were much more ruthless than he realized."

"What do we do next?" Miriam asked, "Notify the FBI?"

"The FBI didn't do shit when it happened," Avram said. "What makes you think they'll be at all helpful now?"

"I have another problem with that, Dad," Alanna said. "I took those photos after hours when the clinic was closed, and had to go through a window to get out. If you show them to anyone, I could get into trouble. Besides, how can we prove that the robot is your design? I thought the thieves took all the plans."

"Not quite," Avram said. He wheeled across the room and reached up to remove a landscape oil painting from the wall. There was a small safe behind it.

"I'll get it, dear," Miriam said as her husband strained in his chair to reach the combination lock. She opened the safe and removed its contents, placing them on her husband's desk.

"I kept an extra backup of all the hardware design at

home," Avram said. "Nobody bothered to ask me, although, to be fair, I was in Intensive Care at the time, recovering from the bullet wound. By the time I left the hospital, DARPA had scrapped the whole project, and the Army put me on retirement and disability. It was clear no one thought a paraplegic could head up a research team to resurrect what had been stolen."

"So, you could prove, in court, that those designs were yours?" Alanna said.

"I think so, if we could get legal custody of the robot. That's the problem."

Alanna walked over to the fireplace and put on another log.

"There's something else I haven't told you." She filled them in on everything that had happened at Los Angeles Memorial, from the death of Belinda Lancaster to the brutal murder of Lisa Keating by the so-called 'Surgeon.'

"I haven't put all the pieces together yet. In particular, I don't know if Lisa's death is connected to anything else. Initially, I suspected that Lisa had been responsible for the two deaths and that someone had killed her to keep her quiet. I thought perhaps she was working for Health Web."

"Is there another possibility?" Avram asked.

"The other possibility, because she was on call all three nights, is that she saw the killer and was killed so she couldn't identify him. In that case, 'The Surgeon' has to be someone on staff at Los Angeles Memorial."

"Or Lisa could have been responsible for the deaths at the hospital, and her death completely unrelated," Miriam said. "She could have been at the wrong place at the wrong time."

"I think what your mother is saying is more probable,"

Avram said. "The killings you describe, believed to be the work of 'the Surgeon,' demonstrate the mind of a vicious psychopath. The ones at the hospital are subtle and medically sophisticated. They were meant to pass as accidental."

"Everything I know about serial killers, I learned from reading mystery novels," Alanna said. "The Surgeon has a unique style of murder. Serial killers always leave a signature, and his is a botched surgery."

Of course," Avram said, "he could still be at Memorial and could have killed Lisa for some entirely different motive that we don't yet know."

"In any case," Alanna said, "Health Web seems to be embroiled in any number of illegal activities. The question is, how can we prove it?"

"Alanna, these people are dangerous," Miriam said. "You've got to promise me you won't go sneaking around anyplace you don't belong. You're my child, and I would die if you were hurt." Her eyes filled with tears.

Alanna put an arm around her thin shoulders and held her. Miriam had been through so much over the past four years.

"Don't worry, Mom. I'm no heroine. What I had in mind, if it's okay with you, Dad, is coming clean with Detective Mosher, the guy who's in charge of the investigation into Lisa's death."

"I think talking to him is a good idea," Miriam said.

"I've already told him what I know or suspect about Lisa, but I didn't say anything about Electra. I wanted to see you first and confirm that it was your design. Mosher seems like a smart guy. Maybe he can expand the investigation and get hold of the robot for us."

Avram grinned. "It's fine with me, honey. Just do me a favor. Don't tell him how you got those photos. Your mother would be very embarrassed to have a jailbird for a daughter."

75

February 15, 1996, 8:00 a.m.
Washington, DC

MOSHER WAS FEELING IMPATIENT. HE'D SPENT the better part of the previous afternoon persuading a judge to issue a search warrant for Magnussen's apartment. The next morning, Mosher and his men stood outside the apartment manager's office armed with the warrant and some excellent photographs of Lisa Keating.

Magnussen's hideaway was in a small, contemporary apartment building in Westwood, south of Wilshire. The neighborhood, over the past several years, had become primarily Iranian, with Persian grocery stores, restaurants, and other businesses gradually occupying the southern part of Westwood Boulevard.

A pair of glass double doors led into a well-kept lobby with an elevator. The manager's apartment was on the ground floor. A sign said "Manager" in English and Farsi. A young man in jogging clothes opened the door.

"Police," Mosher said, holding up his identification. "Are you the manager?"

The man's face paled visibly. "What's wrong? Has there been an accident?"

"No. Nothing like that."

The manager relaxed. "Come in, please."

Mosher motioned his men to stay outside and stepped into the apartment.

"I won't keep you from your run. I have a search warrant here for apartment 3C. It's part of an ongoing investigation. I need the keys."

The manager held out his hand for the document. His lips puckered as he attempted to decipher the legal language. Finally, he handed it back to Mosher and retrieved the key from a kitchen drawer.

"Here is the pass key. Please return it when you are done."

Mosher nodded. "Have a look at these, will you? Tell me if this woman looks familiar. Have you ever seen her around the building?"

He held the photos to the light and gave Mosher a man-to-man smile. "Good-looking woman. I think I have seen her here, once or twice."

"Can you remember when?"

He shook his head. "At night, I think, but I can't remember exactly when. We never spoke."

"Was she alone, or with someone?"

"Alone, when I saw her."

"Thanks," Mosher said. "You can go for your run now. We'll be a while."

The police team took the elevator to the third floor.

"Roth and I will search in here," Mosher said. "The rest

of you, canvass the neighbors in the other apartments and see if anyone recognizes Lisa Keating's photograph."

Magnussen's apartment was a cheerless, furnished one-bedroom with beige carpeting, a cheap matching living room suite upholstered in beige and brown fabric, and a wood coffee table covered with dust. There were no accessories or even magazines to suggest anyone ever used the room.

The breakfast room and kitchen were also lifeless. Magnussen had not bothered with dishes, pots, or cutlery. The refrigerator contained a bottle of sparkling water, a lime, and ice cubes.

The bedroom showed a few more signs of life, a large king-sized bed, beautifully made with expensive embroidered linen and large puffy pillows. The bedside tables had an alarm clock on one side and a radio on the other. The drawer was empty except for a large package of condoms. The closet contained two identical, freshly ironed shirts on hangers and two white terry cloth bath robes. The top drawer of the otherwise empty dresser had a few pairs of men's undershorts.

The bathroom was equally clean and supplied with fluffy white bath towels. In the medicine chest, Magnussen kept a shaver, deodorant, and a bottle of extra-strength Tylenol. The trash basket was empty.

"Quite a setup for a quick screw," Roth said. "Looks like the maid's been here and cleaned up thoroughly since the last time he used this place. I doubt we'll have much luck with fingerprints, but we'll try."

Mosher nodded. "It sure doesn't look like he did any surgeries here. I can't imagine how he could have cleaned up all the blood. He's got to have another place."

"If it's him."

The doorbell rang, and Roth let in one of the patrolmen, who was looking triumphant.

"We've got a witness. The lady next door recognized Dr. Keating's photograph. She said she saw her here several times. She's certain the Doctor rode upstairs in the elevator with her on the night of her son's school play. She checked her calendar for the exact date. Lisa Keating came here to see Magnussen the night she died."

"Great. Roth, take a tape recorder and get a statement from the neighbor. That bastard lied to us, and I'm going to nail him. Maybe with a witness, we finally have some grounds to bring him in."

76

February 16, 1996, 2:30 p.m.
Los Angeles, California

THE BOEING 757 TAXIED TO THE LAX GATE, AND Alanna retrieved her luggage from the overhead rack. The late afternoon flight had been uneventful, and she had spent it mentally rehearsing her planned conversation with Detective Mosher. By the time the plane landed, she had prepared what she thought was a tight, convincing summary of her findings.

It was already dark as she exited the baggage claim area and boarded the shuttle bus to parking lot C. She hated the long-term parking lot. It was huge, and she had occasional nightmares about forgetting the location of her car and wandering its alphabetized rows for hours, completely disoriented.

As a result, she made a habit of writing the parking location on her plane ticket. The Honda was precisely where she left it, considerably dirtier but with its car phone intact. She threw her bags inside the trunk, climbed in, and locked the doors with relief.

Battling the rush hour traffic, which began at three on the 405 Freeway and probably lasted till midnight, she made it to her building and pulled gratefully into the garage. A snack, a hot shower, and bed, in that order, seemed like a good idea. She wouldn't tell anyone she was back. She said she would be gone till Monday, and a day or two to catch up and relax seemed like heaven.

She took the elevator to her floor and stepped out. The hall light was out, and the short corridor felt dark and menacing. She propped the elevator door open with her suitcase, found her keys by the elevator light, and inserted her house key into the door lock using her sense of touch. She was certain she'd double-locked the door when she left for the airport, but the key turned too easily to undo the bolt. She twisted the knob, flung open the door, and flicked the hall light on.

The place was in shambles. Her couch cushions were ripped to shreds, stuffing strewn everywhere. Pictures had been taken off the walls, books knocked off shelves, and papers lay all over the floor. Terrified, she backed out, ran for the elevator, and took it to the ground floor and the safety of the manager's apartment.

She knew Mosher was a homicide detective, but his card was the first thought she had and the first thing that came to hand. He was in his office and took her call. Mosher told her he'd be there in twenty minutes and would send a patrol car immediately.

Alanna stayed in the manager's apartment until the patrol car arrived. Once the patrol officers assured her that no one was lurking in her apartment, she went in to look around. The damage was even worse than it seemed at first glance. They'd ripped into her pillows and mattress, emptied every jar in the kitchen and bathroom, scattered her clothes, and upended all her drawers. It felt like rape.

"What do you think they were looking for?" Mosher asked as he came into the living room and looked around. "You wouldn't happen to have a stash of diamonds or cocaine?"

"Very funny. If I did, I wouldn't be stupid enough to keep it in my apartment," Alanna said, too angry for tears. "I don't have anything worth stealing!"

"Money? Jewelry? Computer?"

"I have a few pieces of good jewelry. Most of it is costume, and none was taken as far as I can tell. I don't keep money in the house. My computer and my TV are still here. They went through my desk, took all the files from the file cabinet, and threw them on the floor. I can't imagine what they thought I was keeping in there."

Mosher walked around, looking in all the corners, careful not to touch or disturb anything.

"This isn't a typical smash-and-grab break-in. Most burglars break in, take the jewelry, the money, and the electronics, and split. They don't rip furniture to pieces. These guys were looking for something specific. Was there anything from the hospital, or connected with the information you gave me, that they could have found?"

Alanna shook her head. "I don't have anything from the hospital unless...." She got up and walked to the hall closet.

"You holding out on me?" Mosher asked.

The camera was on the floor, its back opened as if someone had been searching for film. She bent forward and felt a hand grip her shoulder.

"Don't touch. You might mess up some prints."

"There were some photographs," Alanna said. "I was

going to tell you about them as soon as I'd shown them to my father and confirmed I was right about what they depicted. They're not from the hospital, though."

Mosher loosened his grip and guided her to the kitchen, picking up an overturned chair from the floor.

"Sit down, Doctor. I know you're having a hard time. Let me get out a tape recorder, and you tell me everything. I'll listen."

Alanna opened her purse and pulled out the photos she had taken. She handed them to Mosher, began with her father's medical robotics project at DARPA, and ended with her moonlighting job for Health Web and her recognition of the robot. She left out the part about breaking into the clinic, but explained the photos taken during her escapade disguised as a patient.

"So let me see if I understand this. You're telling me that Health Web is using robots instead of doctors, and the robot they're using was invented by and stolen from your father."

"That's it in a nutshell. I didn't think anyone recognized me at the clinic that day, but maybe I was wrong. Maybe these are what they were after."

Murray examined the photos before placing them in an evidence bag. "Remind me never to get sick. I can't think of anything I'd like less than being treated by a robot. Why'd your father invent the thing in the first place?"

"He didn't invent it to replace physicians. He created it to enhance the physician's ability. The robot can do things doctors can't do."

"Such as?"

"Such as operating over long distances with the surgeon in one place and the robot miles away, or doing microsurgery that's far more precise than humans are capable of. Robotics has the potential to revolutionize surgery. My father never intended his project to be corrupted by the kind of people who run Health Web."

"You know, I like you. You've got brains and you've got guts. If you ever give up medicine, you might consider a career as a cop."

"Or a cleaning lady." She looked despairingly at the remains of her apartment.

"You can't stay here tonight. You have a friend who can put you up?"

"I can make some calls, I guess."

"Make them now. I'm not leaving you here. Whoever did this could be back. Besides, I want forensics to see if they can lift a few prints."

"Can you help get hold of the robot? Seize it as evidence or something. Once my dad and the rest of the DARPA team get hold of it, they can prove it's theirs. My father has the original plans for the electronics in his safe."

"I can try. Where is this place, by the way?"

"Santa Monica. On Wilshire."

"I'll call the Santa Monica P.D. They owe me a few. You know, everywhere I turn, the name Health Web seems to come up. Did you know Lisa Keating's father works for them? He's Vice President or something."

"I didn't know, but it fits somehow. It would have given her a motive."

"For murder? You think she was responsible for Belinda Lancaster and Suzanne Saunders? You think she was capable of murder?"

Alanna weighed her words. "I hate to badmouth someone dead, but if I were a psychologist, I'd call Lisa a sociopath. She was a user, completely self-centered, motivated only by what was good for Lisa. People like her don't feel bound by the usual restraints that govern normal behavior. Yes, I think she was capable of it. I confess I had begun to suspect her, but I couldn't understand her motive."

Mosher pushed himself up from the table. "You may be right, but keep it to yourself for now. Until we solve this case, you're in danger. If it were up to me, I'd send you home to your mother."

Alanna reached for the phone. "I'm due back at work on Monday."

She dialed Gabrielle Broder's home phone number and listened until the machine came on. There was no point in leaving a message. Gaby lived only two blocks away and would be her first choice for a crash pad.

She tried Labor and Delivery and learned that Dr. Broder was on call and in the middle of a delivery. She left a message. Maybe Gabi had a spare key under a flower pot. About five minutes later, the phone rang.

"Gaby?"

"Alanna? It's Larry. I'm glad I caught you at home. The police have been to see me. I wanted to talk to you."

"Larry, it's a bad time. My apartment's been burglarized. The police are here with me, and I'm waiting for a call back from Gabrielle Broder. I'm hoping to spend the night at her apartment."

"If you can't reach Broder, you're welcome to crash on my sofa." He hung up before she could respond.

The forensic tech arrived and began to search for fingerprints.

"Are you planning to cover my entire house and all my possessions with black gunk that doesn't come off? I can't afford to replace everything I own and have my entire apartment painted because you want some prints. If the thieves were smart, they would wear gloves. Cut it out," Alanna yelled.

"Calm down. I'm just having him dust around the knobs and doors, and on your camera. It'll come off with Lysol."

"Thanks a lot. There's nothing I'd rather do with my weekend than spend it scrubbing my cabinets with Lysol."

Alanna stalked into the bedroom, picked up the clothes tossed on the floor, and put them on her bed. Then she emptied her overnight bag into the clothes hamper and packed a few things to take with her. Careful not to disturb the closet door, she hung her clothes on hangers.

"I know my closet needs cleaning, but this wasn't what I had in mind."

When the doorbell rang, Mosher answered it. He let Larry Rosen in and told him not to disturb anything. After a few minutes of explanation, Larry took Alanna's suitcase, and they left the police to finish their work.

Glancing down the hall while they waited for the elevator, she wondered if she would find her door covered with yellow crime scene tape in the morning.

February 16, 1996, 6:30 p.m.
Los Angeles, California

GABI HADN'T CALLED BACK, AND ALANNA decided to take Larry up on his offer. She didn't want to be alone tonight in a strange house, having nightmares.

"No worries. I'm happy to host you. Let's go. You need to get some rest."

Larry pulled his car away from the front of her building, and Alanna leaned back, closing her eyes, trying to soothe the agitation she felt and fighting the tears that threatened to spill over. Why had she even bothered to come back here? She wished with all her heart that she was back in Washington, safe in her room with Mac wagging his tail at the foot of her bed.

78

———

February 16, 1996, 7:30 p.m.
Los Angeles, California

THE SMALL HILLSIDE STREET OVERLOOKING Santa Monica Canyon had several rustic homes perched on pylons in defiance of the possibility of an earthquake. Larry's house was a small one-story contemporary of weathered gray shingle with white-trimmed windows. Alanna imagined, during the day, the view over the canyon would have been lovely, but at night, all she could see from Larry's plate-glass living room windows was an expanse of black with a few twinkling lights.

The living room was cozy, with wood paneling, a fireplace, and built-in bookshelves, loaded with a haphazard assortment of books and magazines, but sparsely furnished.

"I bought the house a few months ago," Larry said. "I haven't had the time or the money to furnish it. However, I do have a convertible sleep sofa in the study."

"Does it make you nervous at all, living perched on the edge of the canyon? What if there's another earthquake?"

"This house survived the last one rather well. According to the geologist, the pylons are firmly buried in bedrock. Anyway, I like the view."

He left to find her some bed linens, and when he returned with fresh sheets, they made the bed together in companionable silence.

When they finished, she took a long shower and washed her hair, allowing the scalding hot water to relax her muscles. Everything was getting to be too much. She couldn't imagine getting up on Monday morning and going to work as usual. She wanted a new apartment, a new city, and a new profession, not necessarily in that order.

After a while, she shut off the water, towel-dried her hair, and changed into her nightgown. She felt exhausted, and the pullout bed with its fresh-smelling sheets seemed heavenly. As she climbed in and reached for the bedside lamp, Larry knocked on the door.

She told him to come in, and he entered carrying a steaming cup of hot chocolate. His small act of kindness made her want to cry.

"How did you know I'm addicted to chocolate?"

"I've always known it was an X-linked genetic trait."

Bending down, he kissed her gently on the forehead. "Sleep well, Alanna. I'll be just down the hall if you need anything."

She reached for his hand and held it, looking up at his face, and was struck by how lovely it was to have someone there when she needed it the most.

She pulled him toward her and kissed his cheek, feeling a sudden spark between them as she did so.

At just past three in the morning, she woke suddenly to a half-remembered nightmare, not knowing where she was. She sat up in bed, spotted the lights of a digital clock, felt for the bedside lamp, and turned it on. It was okay. She was at Larry's house, and she was safe. She got out of bed and pulled the curtain to look outside. Everything was still pitch black.

Breathing more slowly now, she became aware that her bladder was full, and she tiptoed to the bathroom. She was wide awake now. No point in trying to go back to sleep. Perhaps she could find something to read in the living room.

As she went down the hall, the door to the bedroom opened, and Larry stood there, rubbing the sleep out of his eyes.

"I'm sorry," she said. "Did I wake you?"

He shook his head. He was wearing pajama bottoms, but his chest was bare, and a soft light from his room illuminated him from behind. She could see the silhouette of well-developed muscles but not the expression on his face.

"I wasn't sleeping very well. I heard you get up. Are you alright?"

"I've felt better." She walked toward him until they were within touching distance. "As long as you're up, could you hold me for a while?"

He reached out and she stepped into the circle of his arms, resting her head on the warmth of his chest. She heard him exhale a long breath, and then his arms tightened around her.

They stood that way for a long time, not moving, just breathing in synchronous, quiet breaths. It had been so long since anyone held her like this. His hands began to roam ever so gently down her back, stroking her through the thin cotton of her nightgown. Tilting her face toward his, she offered her mouth, meeting his lips with a kiss that surprised them both with its sudden intensity.

79

February 17, 1996, 6:30 a.m.
Los Angeles, California

ALANNA AWOKE TO BRIGHT SUNLIGHT AND realized she was alone in Larry's bed. The sound of a radio drifted down the hallway, and she could smell the scent of fresh coffee. She got up, wrapped herself in Larry's blue terry bathrobe, and walked down the hall. He was dressed, seated at the kitchen table, and reading the Los Angeles Times, a mug of black coffee in his hand.

She smiled, feeling suddenly shy and uncomfortable. He rose from the table, urging her to sit down, and poured her a cup of coffee. He put two slices of bread in the toaster and set out butter and jam. Then he stood behind her, wrapping his arms around her shoulders and inhaling the scent of her hair.

"I could get to like this."

"Me too," she said. "I think you're spoiling me."

"I'm trying. What are your plans for today? Unfortunately, I have to show up for work."

"I'm going to call Mosher and ask if I can start cleaning my apartment. It's bad enough those bastards threw everything I own on the floor, I'm going to have to reupholster my couch."

"That's what you have insurance for," Larry said. "Pick out an expensive fabric and stick it to them. You're welcome to stay here as long as you want to. I imagine it will be a while before you feel safe in your place again."

"If ever. I'll give myself a few days to calm down, but I might need to move."

She put some strawberry jam on her toast and reached for the section of newspaper Larry had abandoned. He left the kitchen, returning with a briefcase and a key chain.

"These are for you, in case you return before I do. I have to prepare a seminar for the residents, so I'll probably be late."

She put down the paper and kissed him.

Alanna finished her coffee in the living room, enjoying the view of the hillside and ocean. She wondered how Larry would feel if she told him the truth about herself and her family. Would he still be interested in a woman who might carry the genes for schizophrenia, a woman who, one day, would have to take complete responsibility for a brilliant, insane sibling?

She usually avoided thinking about the fact that Miriam and Avram wouldn't be there forever. She would care for Sammy. She knew she would when the time came--whatever it took. He was her big brother, and she loved him. Sometimes she wondered what her life would have been like if Sammy had been normal, if he'd finished medical school and become a surgeon as her father had planned for him.

Would she have done something different with her life?

Had she become a physician because of some unconscious need to compensate her father? If so, it hadn't worked. It seemed that Avram barely noticed she had been the one to follow in his footsteps. Why did she feel that nothing she did would ever be good enough for him? Was that why she'd taken such risks to recover his robot? Was it just a bid for attention?

Reluctantly, Alanna forced herself up from her chair. She had other things to worry about now. The self-analysis would have to wait. Rinsing her cup, she dressed and put in a call to Mosher.

"Well, we got one usable print off your camera. He must not have been able to open it with his gloves on. We're running it through the database as we speak."

"Great. Maybe you can catch this guy, and I can return to my life. Is it okay if I go clean up in there this morning?"

"Yeah, but be careful. I wouldn't spend the night there yet. I left your keys with the manager."

"Thanks. Let me know if you manage to catch the guy who broke into my apartment."

"You'll be the first to know," Murray promised.

80

February 17, 1996, 8:00 a.m.
Los Angeles, California

MOSHER HUNG UP THE PHONE AND RETRIEVED the tape of his conversation with Alanna the previous night. He wanted to listen to it one more time. He was starting to feel quite fond of the doctor. Even though she was meddlesome and foolhardy, playing detective the way she had, he found himself admiring her spunk. It also helped that she was as smart as a whip.

Unlike most amateurs who poked their noses into police business, Alanna had made a significant contribution to the case. Most of all, Alanna reminded him of Michelle. Of course, if Michelle had pulled the kind of stunts Alanna had, Mosher would have been far less indulgent.

He began to play the tape, listening to her voice and taking notes. His detective's antenna was certain that it all fit together. If he could only find a few missing pieces, the picture would emerge.

Mosher picked up the phone again and called his friend at the Santa Monica Police Department.

"Murray Mosher here. I need a favor. Are you familiar with the Health Web walk-in clinic on Wilshire? I need one of my boys to look it over. There may be some evidence there pertaining to a big case we're working on."

"You got a warrant?"

"Not yet. I want to check it out first. If the stuff is there, I'll get a warrant. It's a big instrument with three dangling arms. Impossible to miss."

"I can get you in there. They had a break-in about a week ago. We can send someone back there for a follow-up. Just send your guy over and I'll take care of it."

"I owe you," Mosher said, hanging up.

Mosher dispatched one of his patrolmen to Santa Monica with a photograph of the robot and took out all his files on The Surgeon. His intuition told him that Magnussen was responsible, but intuition wasn't adequate for an arrest, let alone a conviction.

This case had a frustrating lack of good forensic evidence. On the plus side, he had a witness linking Lisa Keating to Magnussen's apartment on the night of the murder. He also had a motive, although Keating's confidences to her lawyer were hearsay evidence and not admissible.

He would have to get Magnussen to admit to the affair or obtain a specimen and match his DNA to that of the pregnancy tissue to establish paternity. What he didn't have was a link between Magnussen and the other victims or any clue as to where the actual murders had been committed. It was obvious that they had taken time and some medical expertise.

Mosher wondered if the Surgeon had anesthetized his victims himself or if he had an accomplice. Should he bring Magnussen in for a fishing expedition and possibly warn him, or should he wait until he had something more solid?

81

———————

February 17, 1996, 9:00 a.m.
Los Angeles, California

ALANNA DROVE TO THE FRONT OF HER apartment house, debated pulling into the garage, and decided she would feel safer parked on the street. She pulled her Honda up behind a black Dodge Caravan, set the parking brake, and rang the manager's doorbell. He retrieved her keys and insisted on escorting her safely into her apartment.

In the light of day, the apartment looked even worse than it had the previous night. The police, despite their promise to be careful, had left black fingerprint powder everywhere. Somehow, she doubted that Lysol would do the trick.

She started in the bedroom, hanging and folding her clothing, replacing her possessions in dresser drawers, and taking inventory to be sure she hadn't overlooked anything missing. She tossed used linens and towels into the laundry hamper, threw out the opened jars and bottles of cosmetics that littered the bathroom floor, and vacuumed all the mattress and pillow stuffing that clung to her carpet.

The mattress with its knife slashes was unsalvageable, as were her down pillows. She'd have to ask the manager to help her take them all down to the dumpster in the alley. She started a list of the items she'd have to replace and photographed each room with a new roll of film to document her losses for the insurance company. Touching the items made her feel contaminated. She might have to send all her clothes to the cleaners before wearing them again.

After finishing in the bedroom, she tackled the kitchen, once again throwing out every food item the burglars had touched and scrubbing the floor, sink, and countertop until the kitchen was spotless. Looking at her watch, she was surprised to discover it was already late afternoon. She was exhausted, hungry, and completely daunted by the prospect of tackling her disordered books and papers. It could wait until tomorrow.

She'd stop at the supermarket, pick up some dinner things, and cook something for herself and Larry. It was the least she could do after all his kindness. Maybe she could make time for a short run. Some exercise might make her feel better.

Hoisting the brown plastic garbage bag over her shoulder, she double-locked her door and headed to the basement.

82

February 17, 1996, 4:30 p.m.
Los Angeles, California

T HE TWO MEN INSIDE THE DODGE CARAVAN waited patiently. The van was littered with fast food wrappings and smelled of smoke from the cigarettes the pockmarked man was puffing.

"We should have followed her inside and nabbed her in the apartment."

His companion, a skinny black man with hair in dreadlocks, shook his head.

"Too risky. People have been going in and out of the place all day. She'd be on the phone, dialing 911 before we could pick the lock. She'll come out eventually, and we'll tail her to where she's staying. Then we'll nab her."

"Can I do her before you question her?" The man stubbed out his cigarette and stretched in his seat, thrusting his hips forward suggestively.

"Jesus, Beau. Don't you ever give your dick a rest? You

can do her as many times as you want, before and after I question her. When we're done, the boss wants to see her."

Beau grinned, revealing tobacco-stained teeth. "The boss's taste seems to be improving. I could get to like this part of the job. You wanna do her too, Jimmy?"

Jimmy shrugged. "Fucking white chicks doesn't turn me on much. I'll watch."

"Hey, she's coming out."

Jimmy straightened up and inserted the car key into the ignition. He watched in his rearview mirror as Alanna entered her car and started the engine. He waited until she pulled ahead of him and made a right turn at the corner before he followed. Beau whistled and lit another cigarette.

83

───────────

February 17, 1996, 5:00 p.m.
Los Angeles, California

As Alanna turned off Channel Drive and up the hill to Larry's place, she glanced in her rearview mirror and noticed a black van turning along with her. There had been a similar car parked on her street, but she was being paranoid. Black vans were as common as blonde surfers in Southern California.

She slowed as she approached Larry's driveway and turned in. The black van sped on past her and disappeared as the street curved sharply to the left. Alanna opened the front door, retrieved the bag of groceries she'd picked up at the Von's market on her way, and kicked the door closed behind her. The phone rang as she unloaded her purchases, and she jumped.

"I'm glad you're back. I've been trying for an hour."

"Larry, I'm glad to hear your voice. I just got in." She took a carton of orange juice from the refrigerator and poured herself a glass with one hand.

"I called to tell you I won't be back before ten or eleven. They stuck me with a VIP autopsy."

She caught her breath. "Not another board member?"

"Nah. Entertainment executive. Looks like chronic liver failure secondary to too much booze and too little restraint."

"Too bad," Alanna said. "I just bought all the fixings for lasagna."

"You are breaking my heart. How about we have it tomorrow?"

"Deal. I'll see you later."

She hung up the phone and finished her juice. It was still light and pleasantly cool. Since she didn't have to cook dinner, she'd take a run. She didn't jog often, but the hills were pretty and there wasn't much traffic. It would help the tension subside.

She washed her face and pulled her hair back into a ponytail. Then she changed into shorts, a T-shirt, and her athletic shoes, pinning the house key to her waistband. When she walked past the kitchen, a sudden sound of shattered glass stopped her.

A hand reached through a pane of the back door and reached for the knob. The two men standing there were easily visible through the four glass panels. The hand belonged to a skinny black guy. The one next to him was stocky, pockmarked, and ugly.

The knob didn't turn. The door lock required a key from both sides. The big guy knocked out a second pane, leering at her. It was only a matter of moments before they knocked out all four, splintered the wood, and climbed in. Alanna sprinted for the front door, heart racing, chest heaving. Slamming the door behind her, she started downhill. She could hear footsteps behind her as the men ran along the side yard and emerged into the street less than half a block behind her.

"I'll get the car," she heard one of them yell.

She ran faster, seeing no cars and no one to whom she could turn for help. She had to make it to Channel Drive before they caught up with her. There was a lot of traffic there. They wouldn't dare attack her in full view of a line of motorists.

Behind her, she heard a squeal of tires. She risked a quick look. The van was racing down the street, gaining on her. She ran around a curve and saw traffic a short block ahead. She could feel the sweat pouring down her face and the pain that was now coming with each breath. Only her terror kept her moving. The van appeared, close behind her.

She dashed into the traffic, causing brakes to squeal and horns to honk. If she could only make it across the street. It would be impossible for them to make a turn in all the traffic, and she thought she could elude them if only she could reach the steps.

The famous stairs from Channel Drive to Adelaide were the joy of the aerobic workout crowd. On weekends, a long line of fanatics climbed them at top speed. At this hour, they were almost deserted. She saw the van give up trying to turn left and make a right turn. They'd have to find a parking spot before they could follow her on foot. As she lost sight of them, she began to climb.

The pain in her lungs was almost unbearable, a combination of being badly out of shape and breathing polluted air. Her aching legs could barely lift her. She ran, two steps at a time with a quick pause to breathe, and forced herself to move on. She was three-quarters of the way up when she spotted the men below her. If they caught up with her, she was going to fight.

With an aching burst of speed, she made it to the top. A setting sun was turning the sky an indelible shade of red. Down the street, she spotted an elderly lady with a straw hat and a basket picking roses in her front yard. Alanna jogged toward her.

"Please," she said, between heaving breaths. "Two men are chasing me. They tried to break into my house. Will you let me call the police?"

The woman looked at her suspiciously for a moment, but must have recognized the genuine fear on Alanna's face. She motioned Alanna to her front door and double-locked it, drawing the heavy drapes to her living room window. Peering through a crack in the curtains, Alanna saw her pursuers reach the top of the stairs. They separated, glancing down driveways and behind parked cars, looking for her.

The elderly lady handed her a glass of water and a portable phone. Alanna collapsed into a chair and dialed 911.

84

February 17, 1996, 6:00 p.m.
Los Angeles, California

"Bingo!" Roger Roth entered Mosher's office and slapped a rap sheet onto his desk. "We got a match to the print."

"No shit." Mosher looked at the face on the sheet. Black male, shaved head, wide nostrils, high cheekbones, narrow face, cold eyes. "James Roberts, aka Jimmy Riker, John Rich, Jahal Mohammed. Wanted for parole violation in Texas. Paroled in 1991 after serving five years of a ten-year sentence for armed robbery and manslaughter. Nice piece of work."

"I called the authorities in Dallas. James here disappeared in 1992. No one's been able to track him since. They told me he became quite a computer whiz kid when he was in prison."

"Nice work," Mosher said. "Now all we have to do is find him."

The smile on Roth's face grew wider. "It gets better. There just happens to be a black Dodge Caravan registered to a Jahal Mohammed." He produced a copy of the driver's license with a flourish.

Mosher compared the photographs. Mohammed had long dark hair in dreadlocks, but the face was unmistakable. "Have you already checked out this address?"

"I've sent two guys out with an arrest warrant and put out a city-wide crime information broadcast on the car. We'll get him. He's made two bad mistakes already. That means he's overconfident. You think he's The Surgeon?"

Mosher shook his head. "No, but I think he'll be able to finger the guy for us. I've always thought that The Surgeon had a henchman."

"What do you think he wanted in Dr. Davidson's apartment?"

"I wish I knew, but until we've got this guy behind bars, she's in danger."

The intercom buzzed, and Mosher hit the speaker phone button. "It's the Santa Monica Police Department," the secretary's voice said. "They've got an Alanna Davidson down there, asking to speak to you."

85

February 17, 1996, 6:30 p.m.
Los Angeles, California

THE POLICE ARRIVED AT THE ELDERLY LADY'S house with admirable promptness. Alanna told them her story and accompanied them in the patrol car to Larry's home, where they examined the broken windows, looked for footprints and tire tracks, and waited while Alanna retrieved her small suitcase from the guest bedroom and put it in the trunk of her Honda. They called for a crime team to check the scene, and as soon as the technicians arrived, they told Alanna to follow them in her car to the Santa Monica station.

She knew she couldn't stay at Larry's, and she was frightened for him as well. Who knew whether the two men would return? When they arrived at the station, she asked for a phone and called the hospital page operator. It seemed forever before Larry answered his beeper.

"Larry, something awful happened. You can't go home!"

"Are you hurt?"

"No. My charley horses have charley horses and I may never walk again, but other than that, I'm fine."

"What happened?"

"Two men followed me from my apartment to your house and tried to break in. I ran, and they followed."

"Where are you now?"

"I managed to get to Channel Drive and up the stairs to Adelaide before they could catch me. I called the police. I'm at the station, but I'm afraid for either of us to spend the night at your house. What if they come back?"

"Alanna, I'm so sorry. I'll come get you."

"You're sorry. I'm a jinx. You were nice to me, and you got your house broken into. I've put you in danger, and I feel terrible. Don't come now."

"Why not?"

"I'll be with the police for a while. Then I'll call a hotel and check in. I'll call and tell you where I am. You're invited to spend the night at my expense."

"Okay. I'll arrange for my security service to keep a close eye on the house tonight. Beep me as soon as you've checked in somewhere."

Her next call was to Shutters on the Beach, where she reserved a double room for later, and then she phoned Mosher.

"What are you doing at the station, Doc? You in trouble?"

"Not at the moment," Alanna told him, "but I've had a hell of an afternoon. The guys who probably trashed my place followed me to Larry Rosen's and tried to break in. They were obviously after me because they chased me to Channel Drive. I managed to lose them."

"Can you describe them?"

"Skinny black man with long, messy hair and a stocky, ugly white guy with pockmarks. They drove a black van."

"I think we've identified one of them," Mosher said. "Listen, you are not safe. I need you to be somewhere they can't get at you."

"I just made reservations at Shutters. Will that do?"

"Until tomorrow," Mosher said. "Then I want you out of this city till this is over. Get a flight home. You hear me?"

"I hear you. What am I going to tell them at work?"

"Whatever story you can come up with. By the way, my guys checked out that health clinic for you. There's no robot there. Nothing that resembles the picture you gave me. They must have moved it somewhere else. Now put a cop on the line. I've got some information I need to give him."

Alanna handed the receiver to the patrolman, who jotted down the license number and car description Mosher gave him. She heard him relay it to the cars searching the vicinity of Channel Drive for the van.

After she had signed a written statement, they let her go. She drove her car the short distance to Shutters, embarrassed to arrive at the elegant hotel in her sweat-stained running clothes, with her messy hair and no doubt offensive odor.

She entered the luxurious lobby. A pianist played soft music, and beautifully dressed young couples sat enjoying drinks in the lounge. An impassive reservation clerk checked her in. She declined the service of a porter and carried her small suitcase upstairs.

The room was beautifully furnished with an ocean view and a large bathtub. Alanna double-locked the door, filled the tub with steaming hot water, and scrubbed herself and her hair until she felt clean again. Then, wrapped in a large bath sheet, she called Larry and room service, ordering hot soup and a sandwich.

While she waited, she blew her hair dry and put on jeans and a black turtleneck sweater, the only clean clothes she had left. Despite the hot bath, her joints ached from the unaccustomed exercise, and her pulse was still racing. The two men might have raped or killed her. She had been extraordinarily lucky and, much as she didn't want to admit it, Mosher was right. She should go home to Washington. She didn't want to think about it now. The whole thing was too upsetting.

Room service knocked. The waiter served her supper on an elegant cart. She tipped him and ate, looking out at the view and trying to calm down.

Why had the two men been after her? Did it have to do with the murders at the hospital, or was it somehow tied in with her father's robot, the robot that had suddenly gone missing? Where could they have taken it?

Getting up from her chair, Alanna checked the bedside table for a phone directory. There were two, one for the Westside and one for Los Angeles. She wondered if Health Web had any more clinics in the area. Perhaps the robot had been moved to one of those.

She searched under Physicians, Hospitals, Clinics, and Medical. She found the Health Web clinic in Santa Monica, but no others were listed. There was, however, another listing under Medical Supplies. Health Web had a supply company in the City of Commerce. Perhaps they had taken the robot there. She would mention it to Detective Mosher in the morning.

86

———

February 17, 1996, 9:30 p.m.
Los Angeles, California

AS SHE UNPACKED, ALANNA NOTICED SHE HAD no toothbrush and no clean underwear. She was afraid to go back to her apartment, but perhaps she could take a quick run downstairs. The hotel convenience store might still be open, and she could pick up some toothpaste and a hairbrush.

The lobby was empty and quiet. The pianist had stopped playing. One bored clerk sat dozing behind the front desk. She walked down the hallway past the elevators, but the small store she remembered was closed. Why had she thought it might be open so late?

She should go back to her room and wait for Larry, but she felt too agitated to sleep. There was a Seven-Eleven on Wilshire that was open, and it was only a five-minute drive. She searched in her waist pack until she found her parking receipt and handed it to the valet at the front door.

He brought her Honda, and she slid into the seat,

locking the doors and windows. She pulled out of the driveway and made a left onto Ocean. The streets were deserted. Even the homeless were sleeping peacefully at the Southern end of Santa Monica's Palisades Park.

She made a right turn onto Wilshire, kept her eyes open for the market, and pulled into the parking lot in front of its entrance. Five minutes later, she emerged, having purchased what she came for plus a bottle of Benadryl, a mild, over-the-counter antihistamine that made her drowsy and which, she hoped, would help her to get to sleep.

As she inserted the key into her car door, she heard a footstep behind her. She turned, too late to stop a pair of powerful arms that gripped her from behind. A hand covered her face with a wet cloth, forcing her to inhale a sickly-sweet chemical that made her feel dizzy and disoriented. She twisted wildly, lashing her head from side to side, and kicked back, feeling the heel of her shoe connect with her assailant's knee.

"Fucking bitch!"

He held her with increased strength, immobilizing her arms and forcing the cloth into her mouth.

87

February 17, 1996, 9:30 p.m.
Los Angeles, California

THE POLICE ARRESTED JAMES ROBERTS, AKA Jahed Mohammed, at home, then took him to Parker Center to wait for Mosher.

Mosher and Roth, tape recorder in hand, entered the interrogation room and sat opposite him. The policeman who had been guarding him withdrew. Mosher switched on his tape recorder, gave his name, rank, and the date, and informed Roberts of his rights. Roberts declined an attorney.

"State your name," Mosher said.

"Mohammed, Jahed Mohammed."

"Is this your driver's license, Mr. Mohammed?" Mosher slid it across the table.

"What if it is?"

"You own a black Dodge Caravan?"

"What if I do?"

"Where is it?" Mosher said.

"I dunno."

Mosher saw this would go nowhere and decided to speed things up.

"We know you're wanted in Texas for violating parole."

"You wasting all those cops to get me for that?" Jimmy said, giving him a disgusted look. "Man, I'm not bothering anybody. I live a quiet life. I got a job. Go catch some gang-bangers."

"What were you looking for when you broke into Dr. Davidson's apartment?" Mosher asked.

"I don't know any doctor."

"We got your fingerprints at the scene," Roth said.

"You made a mistake." A thin sheen of sweat broke out on Jimmy's forehead.

"Who are you working for?"

"I don't know who you're talking about," Jimmy said. "I don't wanna talk no more. You get me that lawyer."

Mosher shut off the tape with a sharp flick of the switch. He leaned over the table and went nose to nose with Jimmy, smelling the sharp scent of sweat and fear.

"Listen to me, you fucker. This business involves murder. I got enough on you to put you back for life, and then some. Your only chance is to tell us who you're working for. You think about it."

He motioned to the guard to take Jimmy back to the holding cell and slammed his fist onto the table.

"Call Dr. Davidson. We'll put him in a lineup. Maybe she can identify him. Go downstairs and get me his possessions."

Before he left, Roth tried Alanna at Shutters, but there was no reply. Then he went downstairs and signed out the bag containing Jimmy's jeans, a T-shirt, an expensive Rolex watch, and a wallet. The wallet was thin and made of Italian leather. It contained fifteen dollars, a driver's license, an electronic parking card, and a paycheck stub from Health Web Medical Supplies.

88

February 17, 1996, 10:30 p.m.
Los Angeles, California

ALANNA AWOKE NAUSEATED WITH A SPLITTING headache, lying on something that felt like carpet. The floor vibrated underneath her aching body, and after a moment, she realized she was in a moving vehicle. She groaned, allowing her eyelids to crack open. It was pitch dark.

She opened her eyes fully and waited for her night vision to adjust. It didn't help. Her surroundings remained completely black. Memory returned, and with it a wave of terror. Somehow, they'd found her. They must have followed her to the hotel and waited for her to come out. She would wind up like Lisa Keating, mutilated and dead.

After a few minutes, the nausea subsided, and she forced herself to turn on her side, using her elbows to raise herself into a sitting position. The car swerved suddenly to the right, and she reached out to stabilize herself. When her head stopped spinning, she shifted to her belly, crawling slowly forward to explore the limits of her prison.

She reached a wall, got up on her knees, and searched for a handle, moving systematically to her right, until she found it. She must be locked in the back of a van. Judging by the speed of the vehicle, they were probably on the freeway. Even if she could open the door, she could hardly jump out at sixty miles an hour. But maybe she could find some way to escape once the van stopped. She pushed down gently on the handle to see if it would move. It didn't. She was locked in from the outside.

The car slowed, stopped, and started again in a rhythm that suggested they had left the freeway and were on city streets. Alanna crouched near the door, her hand touching the handle. She would get only one chance when the door opened, and she needed to be ready to move. Her heart pounded as she tried to take deep, slow breaths through her dry mouth and throat. The car stopped. The engine turned off.

Both doors opened simultaneously, and Alanna launched herself from the van, terror fueling her jump. A hand shot out of the darkness and gripped her arm like a vise. There was no mistaking the identity of the cold metal object that pressed her temple, just above her right ear.

"If I hear one sound out of you, it'll be the last one you make. Turn around. Real slow."

The pressure on her arm eased a fraction, allowing her to turn. The man shoved her hard against a wall and jerked her chin up so he could shine a light on her face. His features were in shadow, but she recognized him anyway. It was the pockmarked man. He lowered his light and pushed her ahead of him.

They appeared to be in an industrial area, parked next to a dark, rundown, two-story building. Adjacent to it was a parking lot enclosed in wire fencing. An entrance and a loading dock with a ramp were at the back of the building. A large dumpster stood adjacent to the dock. There was a low row of basement windows with iron bars.

"Get in here."

The man unlocked the door and motioned for Alanna to precede him into the warehouse. The entry led into a dingy stairwell illuminated by a low-watt bulb. Corrugated metal stairs led up. She saw two heavy steel doors, one opposite her and another at the foot of the stairwell.

The man reached into his breast pocket for a security card, which he thrust into a slot beside the knob. Alanna heard a click as the lock released and the door slid open. It was an elevator. He pushed her roughly inside and touched a button labeled B. She could see his face now. Up close, he was even uglier with pale skin, stubby yellow teeth, a half-grown mustache, and cold eyes.

The elevator opened onto a wide corridor with low ceilings and bright fluorescent lights. He used his gun to steer her to the left.

"Why don't you wait for me right here while the boss decides what to do with you? If he doesn't want to see you now, you and I can party." He grinned at her and opened the door to a small room, pushing her inside and locking it behind her.

89

February 17, 1996, 11:00 p.m.
Los Angeles, California

THE PLACE WAS PITCH DARK AND COMPLETELY silent. Once again, the terror that Alanna had been trying to control overwhelmed her. She whimpered like a small, trapped animal, feeling her heart racing and the pulses throbbing in her throat.

Light. That's what she needed. There had to be a switch somewhere. She found it, running her hand along the wall beside the locked door. The room was tiny and windowless. It was some kind of storage closet, only the shelves were empty. She scanned the room for a tool or a weapon. Nothing was lying loose, nothing she could unfasten, no convenient ventilation or air conditioning ducts she could crawl through the way they always did in the movies. Then she remembered her waist pack.

The kidnapper hadn't bothered to search her or to take it from her. Perhaps he hadn't noticed it in the dark, resting on her hip, almost invisible against the black of her jeans and turtleneck. It was large enough for the physician's three essentials: money, keys, and a cellular phone.

Her hand shook as she unzipped the bag, extricated the phone, and pressed the power switch. 911. She could call and tell them she'd been abducted. She pressed the three numbers. **No SVC.** The words lit up at the bottom corner of the digital window. She took a deep breath and counted to ten, waiting for the words to disappear. Nothing.

Something about the basement was cutting off her reception. At the sound of a key turning, she replaced the phone, zipped the pack, and stepped away from the door.

"The boss wants to meet you. He's got a special treat. Move."

He pushed her down the corridor again, to a set of double doors that swung open in response to a plate on the wall. It was an operating room. The familiar metal table stood in the center, its vinyl cushions made up with white sheets, a draped Mayo stand at its foot, an anesthesia machine at its head. Steel cabinets lined one wall, filled with color-coded boxes of suture and disposable surgical instruments.

But that was where the familiarity ended. Another wall contained a huge video screen, the size that yuppies purchased for home theater, along with their Mercedes. Standing next to the operating table was a familiar instrument, ELECTRA. A camera on a tripod stood at the foot of the table. Alanna stared at it, mesmerized.

"Dr. Davidson, how nice to see you. I see you recognize my new toy. How remiss of me not to have made the connection when I first heard your name. Your father developed it, I believe."

The video screen came to life. The smiling face of a red-haired, balding man stared out at her. He wore surgical scrubs and was seated at a video console.

"Who are you?" Alanna asked.

"My name is Brian Drew. Perhaps you've heard of me, or my company, Health Web? I apologize for not being able to be here in person to greet you. I'm in my corporate head-quarters in Dallas. That, however, shouldn't be much of a hindrance. I've been looking forward to demonstrating my system to someone who can appreciate the surgical fine points."

"None of those poor homeless folks I've been practicing on understood what an incredible innovation we have here. I've made a few improvements since I acquired the original."

"You mean stole the original, don't you?"

"Whatever." Drew shrugged. "Imagine, here I am in Dallas, about to use the wonders of telemedicine to operate on you in Los Angeles. Truly a triumph of medical science, wouldn't you say?"

Alanna said nothing.

"Put her on the table, Beau," Drew said.

"No!" Alanna jerked away, taking advantage of the man's momentary lapse of attention to sprint for the door. He had her in a hammerlock a moment later.

"You can get on the table with or without a bullet hole, your choice," Beau said.

"You know, we haven't practiced removing bullets roboti-cally," Drew mused.

"Say the word, boss." He shoved Alanna down on the table, snub-nosed revolver at her neck.

"Perhaps later," Drew said. "I have a few other things in mind first."

Beau tightened a wide strap across her upper thighs. Her

arms were stretched out on the arm boards, Velcro bindings trapping her biceps.

"Haven't you forgotten something, Beau?" Drew asked. "You know it's poor surgical technique to operate on someone wearing clothes. Ruins the sterile field."

Beau grinned, shoved his revolver in his belt, and grabbed a pair of surgical bandage scissors. "Sorry to ruin your outfit," he said.

He cut through the sweater, directly in the midline, and pushed the fabric to either side. A second snip divided the cups of her bra.

"Nice tits." He pinched both nipples hard until she gasped. Then he unbuckled her belt and waist pack, unzipped her, and jerked her jeans and underwear together down past her hips.

"I'd like her prepped and draped now if you don't mind," Drew said.

Alanna felt the ice-cold Betadyne being sponged onto her body. Beau covered her legs with a paper drape and placed another over her neck and arms. Then he uncovered the Mayo stand. Alanna could see additional instrument tips, needle holders, electrocautery, assorted sutures, and a pile of towels and gauze sponges.

"That looks like everything. You can go now," Drew said. "You know I like my privacy when I practice. You can come back and clean up in two hours."

"Have fun," Beau said as he exited the operating room.

"I must apologize, Dr. Davidson," Drew said. "We weren't expecting you. I don't have an anesthesiologist on call tonight. I'm afraid we'll have to do without. Now let's see. I've done a gallbladder and an appendix already. So many choices. A mastectomy might be nice, or perhaps a below-the-knee amputation. What do you think?"

He sat down at his console, and a moment later, the robot began to move.

90

February 17, 1996, 11:00 p.m.
Los Angeles, California

"I GOT IT," ROTH SAID, WAVING THE SEARCH warrant for Health Web Medical Supplies.

"Let's go." Mosher motioned to four other cops in the squad room, and the team jogged to the parking lot, commandeering two squad cars. They pulled out of the station house and headed for the freeway.

"So, what do you expect to find?" Roth asked.

"Maybe nothing. Maybe The Surgeon's operating room. We'll see. My gut tells me we're close and closing in."

91

February 17, 1996, 11:45 p.m.
Los Angeles, California

"WAIT. WHY ARE YOU DOING THIS?" ALANNA asked.

The robotic arms paused, and Brian Drew smiled at her from the video screen. A picture of her terrified face appeared in another window, next to him.

"Oh, just call it clinical trials. After all, I can't install my diagnostic and surgical system all over the country without being certain it works, can I? I wouldn't want to practice bad medicine."

She had to keep him talking. When he spoke to her, the screen showed a close-up of her face, and he wasn't watching her body. As soon as he began to operate, the camera would zoom in on her body.

"Were you doing clinical trials on all those homeless people they found dead under the freeway?"

"Well, yes. The nice thing about the homeless is that no one pays any attention when they die. If you think about it, helping me practice was probably the only useful contribution any of them ever made to civilization."

"Yes, I can see you might view it that way." Alanna strained against the straps on her upper arms. She had to do something to get loose before he turned around again. The straps were tight, but not intolerable. They were designed to keep the arms of an anesthetized patient out of the way of the surgeons, not to restrain a conscious one.

She pulled her arms hard, toward the midline, and she felt a ratchet of the arm board give way. She pulled again. If she could rotate the board ninety degrees, she could reach the strap across her thighs.

"What about Dr. Keating? Did you kill her, too?"

"Ah, Lisa. What a woman. What nerve and creativity. Such a shame to lose her."

The picture on the monitor changed to reveal her chest, and Alanna froze. The robotic arm with the scalpel tip lifted. The scalpel danced over her skin, tracing incisions in the air.

Alanna braced herself for the first cut. It came on her chest, a skin incision that circled her right breast, allowing bright red blood to well up and drip down toward her belly. The cut burned. The robot descended again, tracing a similar line around the left breast. He was toying with her, trying to increase her terror with every cut.

"I can't decide," Drew said. "So many useful surgeries to be tried out."

"Did you give Lisa her choice of operations?" Alanna asked.

"Lisa wanted an abortion. I was happy to comply."

The arm boards were moving. Alanna pulled with all her strength, trying to ignore the pain around her breasts. Each click of the ratchet brought her arm closer to the strap binding her thighs. She bent her right elbow and felt the Velcro edge with her fingers.

"Lisa helped me eliminate the opposition to my takeover of your hospital. Too bad she didn't succeed with Arthur Underwood. That would have been a coup."

"You mean Lisa was the person who almost killed him?"

Alanna slowly undid the strap binding her thighs, hidden under the paper drape. Bending her knees and digging her heels into the mattress, she pushed herself further up the table. The straps on her upper arms slipped down and loosened.

"Of course she was. She also handled the overdose on that narcissistic movie star and arranged for the little accident to Lancaster's wife. Truly, the woman was a genius."

She was free of the straps now. Reaching for the Mayo stand, she grabbed a towel and threw it over the video camera. Her image on Drew's screen disappeared.

Alanna threw off the drapes, sat, and pulled up her jeans. She zipped the jacket of her sweatsuit, covering her bare breasts, and replaced her waist pack.

"Unfortunately, Lisa got greedy. I prefer employees who take orders. Not that I'm opposed to a little initiative, you understand, but too much, at the wrong time, could ruin my plans." His smile was chilling. "What the fuck just happened to my camera?"

"What plans?" Alanna said.

She needed a weapon, and then, she was out of there. Hopefully, he'd think he had a computer malfunction, not a free prisoner.

"I have magnificent plans for your father's invention. Think of how much money it will save. It should generate billions for Health Web."

Alanna scanned the storage shelves on the side of the room, looking for anything useful.

"That wasn't the reason my father and DARPA developed it. It was designed to go into places where there weren't enough doctors; remote regions of the world or battlefields, and to treat people who couldn't reach a hospital."

She found and opened a laparoscopic trocar, a steel spike with a razor-edged pyramidal point, designed to penetrate the abdominal wall. It would have to do.

"Magnanimous, I'm sure, and ideal for the new medicine. I wish your father could see you now. He'd be so proud."

Drew swiveled in his chair, his back toward her.

"Shit. God damn satellite connection!" He punched buttons wildly on his console.

It was time to go before he realized it wasn't his system and called his pockmarked colleague. Trocar in hand, Alanna opened the door a crack and looked both ways. She saw no one. Exit signs winked red at both ends of the corridor. She chose the direction away from the elevator and walked silently down the hall.

A door led to a stairwell, a dim red bulb illuminating the landing. She took the stairs two at a time and found herself in front of a door labeled First Floor. Heart pounding, she paused for breath and remembered her cellular phone. No telling where the pockmarked man might be, and a trocar was no match for a gun. Reinforcements would be welcome.

She pressed the power button on the phone and waited. This time, the **No SVC** sign was blessedly absent. Knowing that Brian Drew was behind it all confirmed her suspicion about where she'd been taken. This is getting to be a bad habit, she thought as she dialed 911.

92

February 18, 1996, 12:00 a.m.
Los Angeles, California

MOSHER AND THE TEAM DRIVING THE TWO squad cars were listening to the police radio dispatch as they sped down the Santa Ana Freeway. The word Surgeon caught his attention, and he turned the volume up.

"Female caller on cell phone claims to have just escaped the serial killer known as The Surgeon. All cars in the vicinity of the City of Commerce converge on Health Web Medical Warehouse. The address is…"

"Step on it!" Mosher shouted.

Roth floored the gas and turned on the police siren as the squad car sped up to ninety miles an hour. The Atlantic Avenue exit was just ahead.

93

February 18, 1996, 12:10 a.m.
Los Angeles, California

BRIAN DREW REBOOTED HIS SYSTEM AND TRIED again to get a visual. Both visual and audio appeared to be offline. Either that or the Davidson bitch wasn't answering. Maybe the problem was at the other end. Beau was no electronic genius, but he'd better have him check it out. Thoroughly annoyed at having his playtime disrupted, the Surgeon reached for the telephone and paged his underling.

"Something's wrong with the damn computer system. Go check the operating room and make sure everything's okay with the robot and the camera."

"Sure, boss. Did you start on the girl?"

"Just a few preliminary incisions. You can play with her while I get the system operational."

Alanna replaced the cell phone in her pack. Try the door. The pockmarked man couldn't be everywhere. Maybe she could slip by him and find an exit.

Alanna opened the stairwell door slowly and peered out. Beau was walking toward her.

"Hey bitch, how'd you get loose?"

She let the door go and sprinted down the stairs. She could hear him coming after her. When she reached the hallway, she began to run toward the elevator at the other end. He was behind her and gaining. His legs were longer, and her knee joints were sending sharp jabs of excruciating pain along her legs as she ran. Warm rivulets of blood dripped down her chest. She glanced over her shoulder. He was only a few yards away. She wasn't going to make it.

Spinning, she sprinted towards him, trocar held firmly in front of her. His momentum carried him forward and impaled him on the spike she drove below his rib cage and into his spleen.

He fell, shrieking with pain. She ran for the open doors of the elevator. As she entered it and turned, she saw him reach for his revolver. She hit the button and pressed herself against the side wall. A hail of bullets ricocheted off the closing steel doors as the elevator began to rise. When it opened on the first floor, she flung herself through the exit door and into the alley. At that moment, two police cars, red lights flashing, pulled up alongside her.

EPILOGUE

May 1, 1999, 1:30 p.m.
Philadelphia, Pennsylvania

THE SESSION ON "EMERGING ROBOTIC Technology in the Operating Rooms of the Twenty-First Century" at the 47th annual meeting of the American College of Obstetrics and Gynecology had been well attended.

Associate Professor Alanna Davidson paused before delivering her final remarks to acknowledge the extended applause that followed her video presentation.

"In summary, the robotics group at Los Angeles Memorial Hospital, in conjunction with DARPA, has completed successful clinical trials using the ELECTRA robotic system. In addition to the gynecologic surgeries I presented, we have completed trials in general, orthopedic, and neurosurgery. Our next step will be to train technical personnel and adapt our system to mobile vans for outreach into medically underserved areas."

"To those who are concerned about robots replacing doctors, I remind you that the robot, like the scalpel, the forceps, or the laser, is merely a tool, an extension of, and never a replacement for, a physician's knowledge, training, and compassion. Thank you for your attention."

Alanna left the stage and walked to the back of the room, where her parents were seated in the last row to accommodate Avram's wheelchair.

"Well done. A chip off the old block." Avram said

"She's prettier than the old block," her husband said.

Alanna slid into a seat beside Larry and relaxed as they listened to the final morning talk. Her father was taking notes and smiling. Avram had smiled often since the robot was recovered and DARPA had reinstituted the project, appointing him as the director.

Alanna accepted a faculty appointment at Memorial after her fellowship and received a DARPA grant to conduct the first clinical trial on ELECTRA. The hospital committee on human research had been skeptical, given the bad publicity associated with the robot, but was persuaded that the killer, not the robot, was at fault.

At Los Angeles Memorial, the new Board of Directors voted unanimously to remain an independent, university-affiliated institution and not to sell out to any profit-making corporation.

They also voted to replace Sherman Magnussen as chair of the OB-GYN department. His staff privileges were canceled after several past residents, nurses, and secretarial employees joined a sexual harassment suit against him.

Brian Drew was arrested in his office by the Dallas police department, transferred to Los Angeles, and convicted of multiple first-degree murders. Alanna's testimony had been a critical part of the trial.

Jimmy and Beau (who recovered from his stab wound)

were both tried as accessories and sentenced to twenty years without parole.

The former Major McGreevy was arrested and convicted of grand theft. The Major admitted to drugging the Colonel's champagne and giving Drew detailed information about the DARPA security system and Avram's location. He vehemently denied having any knowledge that Avram was going to be shot.

The government seized the assets of American Robotics and began an ongoing investigation into the activities of Health Web.

The Davidson family applauded the final speaker and took the elevator to the hotel restaurant.

"I'm glad that's over," Alanna said. "I wonder if you ever stop being nervous before one of those presentations."

"I never did," Avram admitted. "You did a great job, as usual."

"You do seem to be thriving in academic medicine, dear," Miriam said.

"It's a major improvement over working for some HMO," Alanna said. "My next project is setting up a resident training program for remote surgery. It's nice to be excited about what I'm doing."

"Before she starts that," Larry said, slipping an arm around her, "the professor and I need to finish packing. This medical conference is not my idea of a vacation. I have plane tickets to Rome for tomorrow morning. We've scheduled two weeks of Chianti and pasta, and no conversations about the state of medicine."

"Sounds perfect to me," Miriam said.

"It will be," Alanna said. "Fond as I am of your robot, Dad, there are several pleasurable activities I plan to indulge in that still require human beings."

ACKNOWLEDGMENTS

First and foremost, I'd like to acknowledge my wonderful husband, Uri Bernstein, and thank him for cleaning out the garage. Why was this so important? After forty years of using our garage as the repository for things we thought we might still need, we cleared it out to convert it into guest quarters. During the process, Uri came home with a carton of old Hannah Kline manuscripts. I recycled them, because all the novels were already published, but at the very bottom was an early draft of Remote Control, a novel I'd forgotten about.

In 1996, I attended a medical conference in Santa Barbara, hosted by Computer Motion, on New Developments in Robotic Surgery. The demonstration was remarkable, and the audience gave it a standing ovation. I walked out, convinced that I'd witnessed the newest paradigm in surgical technique.

Inspired by what I saw, I wrote Remote Control and gave it to my agent. She tried to sell it but was unable to find an editor who would believe that robotic surgery was possible. I gave up and put the manuscript away.

When I reread it, twenty-eight years later, I recognized that people would now believe in robotics, and after publishing nine novels and scores of short stories, I could make it even better.

I edited it with the help of my longtime, wonderful editor, Linda Schreyer, and my writing group, which includes Darlene Bash, Lori Collister, and Rick Droughten. We have been together for a dozen years, and I can't imagine writing anything without their insightful feedback and friendship.

I'm grateful to Laurie Stevens, my beta reader, for her insightful comments. Laurie is an exceptionally talented thriller writer, and her books are among my favorite reads. My longtime medical partner, Pamela Fenton, checked the manuscript for medical errors. Christiana Miller handled all the formatting and distribution and is my go-to person for marketing guidance. Kristin Bryant, my talented cover designer, is responsible for the cover.

A big thanks to all of you.

Recently, a medical robot, programmed with AI, performed a gall bladder surgery on a pig without any human intervention. The timing was perfect for a novel set at the dawn of robotic surgery. I hope you enjoyed it.

ABOUT THE AUTHOR

PAULA BERNSTEIN is a physician, a scientist, and the author of the medically themed series *Hannah Kline Mysteries*. Her short stories have been included in the anthologies *LAst Resort, Avenging Angelinos, A New York State of Crime, Angel City Beat, Made in L.A., Hollywood Adjacent, and Drop Dead Gorgeous-Daughters of Dread*. They have also been published in Short-Story.me, Fiction on the Web, Persimmon Tree, and Calliope. She has been an active member of Sisters in Crime and served as President of the Los Angeles Chapter and Chair of the California Crime Writers Conference.

Her nonfiction publications include *Carrying a Little Extra, A Guide to Pregnancy for the Plus-Sized Woman* (Penguin), *and Woman to Woman, A Gynecologist's Guide to Your Body* (Bantam).

Learn more about Paula and her books at her website: https://www.paulabernsteinbooks.com/

ALSO BY PAULA BERNSTEIN

The Hannah Kline Mysteries

Murder in the Family

Murder by Lethal Injection

Murder in a Private School

Murder in the Goldilocks Zone

Murder in Vitro

Murder on Her Honeymoon

Murder is a Nightmare

Murder is a Hate Crime

Murder is Paralyzing